Epic Cool

by Diane Farr

Book III of *The Spellspinners*

Other books by this author:

The Nobody

Playing to Win (*originally published as* Fair Game)

Falling for Chloe

Once Upon A Christmas

Dashing Through the Snow (*originally published as* Reckless Miss Ripley *in the anthology* A Regency Christmas Eve)

The Fortune Hunter

Duel of Hearts

Under the Wishing Star

Under A Lucky Star

Wicked Cool

Scary Cool

Information available at <u>dianefarrbooks.com</u>

Dedication

to SUZ DeMELLO

the book midwife

who pulled this one outta me kicking and screaming

Chapter 1

I closed my eyes, pressed my cheek against Lance's shoulder blade, and dreamed of flying. The roar of the bike mingled with the roar of cold wind as we swooped and dived and floated down the long, curving highway, so in sync with each other that we moved as one.

I'd never ridden a motorcycle before, so I had nothing to compare this to. Even so, I knew riding with Lance was way different than riding with anyone else would be. Our minds link the instant we touch, which banished my newbie awkwardness and lent me Lance's ease and confidence. Once we got on the motorcycle, fleeing Spellhaven was smooth as a slow dance. I might have actually enjoyed it, if I hadn't been so cold.

And so jumpy. I kept wanting to peek over my shoulder to see if we were being followed. Which was crazy, of course, because there's no way we were being followed.

The spellspinners' ruling Council didn't need to chase us down the highway. Why bother? They'd track us through other means. Sooner or later, they'd find us.

Lance was throwing a glamour over us as we fled Spellhaven and zoomed toward Cherry Glen. I lent some of my own power to his push, since I figured it was worth the effort. May as well make the Council's job as hard as we could. There was little enough we could do, but a glamour was better than nothing.

I don't mean glamor like Hollywood-type glamor. Glamour is an older word with an older meaning. Among spellspinners, a glamour is a spell that makes you look like something you're not.

Come to think of it, Hollywood glamor does that too.

We didn't have the mojo to do anything elaborate. Luckily for us, night had fallen and it was wicked dark in the forest. So that helped.

We were way past tired.

Plus neither of us had our power stones.

Plus, perched on Lance's bike — at least, I hoped it was his, although I hadn't actually asked — we weren't touching the ground. Spellspinner power rises up from the core of the earth, so physical contact with the planet helps. We were at a disadvantage, even pulling a simple trick like cloaking ourselves in a glamour. We had to do it, though. We looked like refugees from a zombie movie, and without the glamour, a cop might stop us — we weren't wearing helmets. Plus anyone who saw us would remember us. We couldn't afford that.

Being held prisoner in a forest does a number on your personal hygiene. We were filthy from head to toe. Caked with dust, plus streaked with black gunk where the layers of dirt were stuck to us with sap. Under the muck we were wearing the clothes we'd worn to the Homecoming Dance at Cherry Glen High — an event now so far in the past that it was impossible to tell what the original color of my dress was (lavender, for the record). Lance's suit, or what remained of it — pieces were missing — was so trashed that some of it was in shreds. My silk frock had been short to begin with. Now, it barely covered the essentials.

So basically, without the glamour we looked like we just clawed our way out of our graves using our fingernails.

Which, in a way, we had.

I was glad Lance thought of the glamour trick. Sometimes it's nice to have a little spellspinner power on tap.

My thoughts grew increasingly fragmented as we sailed from curve to curve through a seemingly endless, pitch-dark tunnel of redwoods. I was tired of being cold. Tired of feeling hunted. Tired in general. My eyes closed. My mind drifted. It wasn't until I heard Lance's voice in my head, like a sharp shove — *Zara!* — that I realized I was falling asleep.

Wow, that could be dangerous.

Sorry, I sent back, pulling my spine a little straighter. I felt his uneasiness and was embarrassed. *I'm fine. Really.*

He didn't believe me. And with good reason; he had reached the edge of his own endurance, too. I felt him turning possibilities over in his mind, trying to decide what to do.

Let's just keep going, I urged. But he brushed my suggestion aside and continued to think. I wasn't picking up his individual thoughts, but I could sense the wheels turning, so to speak. Then I caught his main idea, which was to pull over at the next likely spot, hide the bike somehow, and crawl off in the woods for a few hours of shut-eye. I shot that down immediately. *No way.*

I felt him agree with me. We'd had enough of the woods for a while, thank you very much, after serving time in Spellhaven.

Then, like a miracle, we swooped around the next bend and encountered civilization — or what passes for civilization in the wilds of the redwood forest: a wide place in the road. On the right, a dimly-lit gas station, a café, and a couple of stores. On the left, a motel.

A motel! For a second or so, I was afraid I'd fallen asleep after all and was dreaming.

Lance swerved across the narrow highway in a graceful arc and parked the motorcycle in a dirt lot, away from the motel entrance. If I hadn't been so tired, I would have found the reasons I saw in his mind amusing. He didn't want the desk clerk to see the motorcycle because (a) motel desk clerks take a dim view of motorcycles and (b) this particular motorcycle was a hunk of junk. Basically, he was ashamed to be seen riding it.

"Come on," he said, helping me off the bike. "Make sure you're awake. This will be harder than just passing people on the road."

"What will be harder? The—" I stopped before saying it aloud. *The glamour, you mean?*

He nodded. *We'll keep it simple. T-shirts and jeans.* I had recently learned that 'aim for the minimum' is Rule Number One when using spellspinner powers, so that's what Lance was asking me to do. He sent me an image of us, appearing slightly older than our current selves, clean and nondescript. *We have to be over eighteen. Don't be nervous.*

I was going to deny it, but there was no point. Lance knew exactly how nervous I was. Wholesoul has its downside.

"You can do this," he said.

I tried to smile. "Piece of cake."

We hiked up the scrubby little hill to the cabin with the OFFICE sign. Lance paused outside the door. "Better ditch the heels, babe. You'll break the glamour if you strut."

"I don't feel much like strutting. And don't call me babe." But I took off my once-spangly pumps. I'd been longing to do that anyhow. As they slid off my heels, they crunched like sandpaper against my skin. Dirt. Pure dirt.

"You sure I should go in there barefooted? My feet are black. I'll leave tracks."

He shrugged. "It won't matter. You're overthinking this."

I'm still new at this spellspinner stuff. I felt like I was about to take my first high dive, without first finding out if I could swim. "Let's make sure we're on the same page," I said. "Send me what you've got."

He locked eyes with me. "Got it?" he said softly.

It's dangerous for me to look too deeply into Lance Donovan's kryptonite eyes. I fell into them like I'd been pushed off the high-dive I'd just imagined. And then floated for a moment, dizzy and weightless.

The effect Lance has on me would be embarrassing, but—thanks to wholesoul—I happen to know I have a similar effect on him.

I pulled myself together and focused on the image he was sending me. A clean, T-shirted Zara. I'd seen that girl in the mirror a million times. I took a deep breath, then painted her over me like a second skin. *Got it.*

"No worries, Zara," Lance murmured, slanting me a wicked smile. "We just pwned every spellspinner in the world. Even the Council. The desk clerk's just a stick."

I rolled my eyes, but felt better. I hate that spellspinners call people who aren't spellspinners 'sticks,' but what can you do? We have to call them something.

We went in. The door squeaked.

A blast of artificial heat smote my chilled skin. The grimy little office seemed stuffy after so many days outdoors, but the warmth was heavenly. We'd entered a narrow room with a cluttered counter at one end. Behind it, a skinny old man with his feet propped up on his desk was watching a sitcom rerun on an ancient portable TV. A wall clock advertising Nehi grape soda pointed at five minutes past eight. I couldn't believe it was so early. Felt like midnight at least.

"Hello," said Lance politely.

"Hiya, kids," replied the old man. "Can I help you?" His sharp eyes darted from Lance to me and back again.

I felt a blush climbing up my neck. I was terrified that he could see right through our feeble little glamour. Was this actually working? Could he really not see how dirty and battered we looked? I'd never before used Power to deceive—with somebody looking right at me, no less. Guilt flooded me.

Lance shot me a quick warning glance. He knew what I was feeling, of course. I dropped my eyes and turned away, pretending to look through the tourist brochures on a rack hanging near the door. *Later,* I promised myself. *I'll think about it later.* Meanwhile, I clung desperately to the image of T-shirt and jeans I was projecting, and ignored my urge to hide behind the fake potted palm.

"Would you happen to have a room with two beds?" Lance asked.

Ah, yes, very clever. We instantly seemed more respectable. I hoped.

"We-el," the man said, "all my double queens is booked. I got one with a queen an' a twin."

"That'll be fine." Lance pulled a billfold out of his back pocket. I was momentarily surprised, but then I thought, why? There was no reason for our Spellhaven jailers to take his wallet. I left my purse back in the Cherry Glen High gym, but life is like that. You know, unfair.

It was reassuring to see how calmly Lance handled the situation. He's only a year older than I am, but in some ways he's a lot more grown-up. Long years of being a loner, I suppose. He paid cash, signed the register, and showed his I.D. — which I sensed him tweak, changing his age from seventeen to twenty. Guess that made me nineteen instead of sixteen.

I picked up a random brochure. DRIVE-THRU TREE, it announced. It featured a garishly-colored photograph of a laughing family in an old-fashioned station wagon, apparently thrilled to pieces to be driving their car through the hollowed-out trunk of a still-living redwood. I felt a pang of sympathy for the mutilated tree. Then I froze. The old man was pointing at me.

"Gotta have your friend's name too, Mr. Donovan," he said.

"That's my sister," said Lance. He lied so well, I almost believed it myself. "Zara."

"Pretty girl," he remarked. "Hiya, Sarah."

No point in correcting him. I forced a smile. "Hullo."

"Two keys or one?"

"Two, I guess."

The old man handed Lance two keys. "Number four," he said. "Enjoy your stay."

I stumbled back out into the cold, dank darkness, weak with relief. We'd pulled it off. I couldn't believe it.

"Believe it," said Lance. He handed me a key. It wasn't a key card, it was an actual key, a metal key on a ginormous plastic tag. "Yeah," he said. "Strictly old school."

Stop answering my thoughts out loud. You'll do it in public someday. We'll be sooo busted.

He grinned. "You're right. Bad habit."

"So knock it off." I picked up my discarded shoes, but couldn't bear to put them on again. I padded down the wooden sidewalk barefooted. As we passed rooms one through three I shivered — and only partly because my bare arms missed the heat. "This place is a dump," I whispered.

Lance agreed. "Looks like the motel in 'Psycho.'"

"Hey, don't say that. I'm about to take a shower."

We were joking, but the Treeside Lodge did bear an eerie resemblance to the Bates Motel. I hoped we'd fare better than the luckless souls who checked in there. The way things had been going lately, I wasn't placing any bets.

Lance unlocked number four and ushered me in to our new digs. I flicked on the light and wrinkled my nose at the old-motel smell.

"Never mind," said Lance. "It'll have a bathroom."

It did. I peeked in. It was small and beat-up, but clean. "Towels," I said reverently. "Shampoo. I can hardly wait." And then I saw myself in the mirror. My eyes widened in horror. "Holy mother of frogs." I looked even worse than I thought.

Lance's face appeared over my shoulder. He looked startled by his reflection too. I pushed him back out the door before he could get any ideas. "Ladies first," I said.

I sensed his grin on the other side of the door. "I'm going to check the shops," he said. "One of them still had its lights on."

"Good idea," I said. "Bring back some crackers or something."

I turned on the taps. The sound of that water thundering into the tub was the loveliest music I'd ever heard. I peeled off what was left of my ruined clothes, stepped into the shower and whimpered with bliss.

"Ah," I said. "Oh." And words to that effect.

Time lost all meaning as the magic of hot water, soap and shampoo temporarily banished my every worry. A thick river of dirt ran down the drain. I think I sang. I was delirious. By the time I returned to my senses I had used every drop of the shampoo and most of the conditioner in the teeny bottles provided by the Treeside Lodge, and the little bar of soap was reduced to microscopic proportions.

Oops.

I turned off the water, feeling guilty. I felt even more guilty when I realized there were only two towels. That didn't stop me from using both of them. Hey, I had nothing to wear.

I was just tucking the second towel into a makeshift sarong (towel number one was tied around my hair) when I heard a key rattling in the motel room door. "Honey, I'm home," Lance called.

Ha, ha.

I opened the bathroom door a crack, sending out a cloud of steam. Lance's arms were full. He dropped the stuff on the sagging twin bed.

I blinked. "Sweatpants?"

His eyes flicked over me. He didn't comment on my getup. But then, since I could tell what he was thinking, he didn't need to.

I blushed. And tried not to let my thoughts go where Lance's had gone.

Have I mentioned that the boy is drop-dead gorgeous? I'd just spent hours trying to ignore it while riding behind him on a freaking motorcycle. Had it been easy? No, it had not, thank you very much.

And now we were alone. In a motel room.

I was deeply grateful that Lance was filthy and ragged at the moment. It definitely helped me keep my equilibrium.

To my relief, he merely answered my question. "They had souvenirs at the convenience store. So, yeah, sweats. Featuring the world famous Drive-Thru Tree." He held up a cheap gray sweatshirt with the tree emblazoned on the front. I burst out laughing and he grinned. "They'll be clean at least."

"Um…you didn't happen to buy any shampoo or towels, did you?"

He picked up the confession in my brain and shook his head in mock sorrow. "Oh, Zara, Zara, Zara."

"I'm really sorry—" I began, but he interrupted me.

"Kidding. This is an easy one to fix." He strolled over to a door in the wall that obviously led to an adjoining room. I hadn't even noticed it. Lance touched the lock and it sprang open.

Spellspinners. What are you gonna do?

He walked into the empty room and returned with its stash of towels, soap and shampoo. I frowned. "That's rude."

"And using all the shampoo while I'm out buying you stuff is—?"

I sighed. "Okay. I'll shut up."

While he was in the shower I put on the smaller of the two sets of sweats he'd bought. They looked ridiculous but felt divine. He'd also snagged a bag of Doritos. I pounced on it and wolfed down about half the bag. There were cookies too, but once the edge was off my hunger, exhaustion suddenly hit me with a wallop.

I stretched out on the queen-sized bed, trying to mentally count the number of times in my life I had been this tired. Came up empty. I reminded myself that spellspinners don't actually need sleep.

Then I rolled onto my side and fell asleep.

I awoke, disoriented, to someone pounding on the door. Lance had fallen asleep behind me with his arm draped across my hip. Not sure how I slept through that. My skin tingled with awareness where his arm lay. The light was still on, so sleep must have ambushed him the way it ambushed me.

"Manager!" shouted an angry voice outside the door. More knocking.

Lance slipped off the bed and went to the door. He was tense and angry with himself, but I wasn't sure why. He sent me one flick of warning— *Quiet* — then opened the door as calmly and politely as you please. "May I help you?"

The skinny old man was out there, standing in the circle of dim light cast by the lamp outside the door. He was clearly furious. "You owe me a hundred bucks, son."

"I do? What for?"

"You slipped me a fast one. I let you pay cash for the room and gave you change for a hundred. You didn't give me no hundred dollar bill." He was waving something in front of Lance's face. "This's a receipt! Just an ol' receipt for a hamburg. Not even a fancy hamburg. Foster's Freeze."

I felt the push go out from Lance's mind. "What are you talking about? That's a hundred dollar bill."

Of course the old man held it aloft to show it to Lance, thinking to prove his point. And of course when he did, he saw that he was holding a hundred dollar bill.

He wasn't. But that's what he saw.

He looked thunderstruck.

"It's late," said Lance. "Maybe you fell asleep. Seems you were dreaming, sir."

What made me sick was he sounded so *nice*. Like he was ready to forgive the motel manager for insulting him. Like he wasn't going to hold a grudge.

The manager's face was turning red. "Well, I can't believe it. I just can't believe it," he said. "Must've fallen asleep, like you said. I saw it plain as plain." He shook his head. "Never done such a thing before in all my born days."

"Could happen to anyone," said Lance. "I used to sleepwalk when I was a kid."

"You're still a kid," said the manager, barking out an embarrassed-sounding laugh. "You sleep tight now. I'm sorry I disturbed you, and that's the truth."

"Good night," said Lance pleasantly. He shut the door as the old man walked away. Then he turned and looked at me. *We have to go.*

"Yeah," I said. The buzz I had gotten from Lance's touch was well and truly gone. So was the illusion of blissful safety the hot water and Doritos had briefly loaned me. I started gathering our tiny stash of belongings. My hands were shaking. "We probably shouldn't have stopped. And by the way, I can't believe you did that."

"Fall asleep while I still had a glamour running? I can't believe I did it either."

He was deliberately misunderstanding me. I was upset about him stealing a hundred dollars from the motel manager. He knew it. And I knew he knew it. And so on. So I said nothing. No point.

I was on the run, in terrible danger, and my only ally was Lance. I had no choice but to trust him. I couldn't do without him. And I hated this reminder that Lance is probably the least trustworthy person I know.

We dumped everything into a plastic bag and I stood in front of the mirror to braid my hair. It was still damp and I didn't want it flying all over the place while we rode.

"We'll pay him back," Lance said at last. "Okay? It was an emergency, Zara. I'll send him his hundred bucks in a few days."

My eyes met his in the mirror. "And where will you get *that* hundred bucks? Don't tell me. I don't want to know."

Anger flashed briefly in his green, green eyes. "This is how money works. Mistaking a piece of paper for something valuable. Right?"

I frowned. "Are you saying there's no difference between a hamburger receipt and a hundred dollar bill?"

"Molecularly speaking? Not much."

He was right and wrong at the same time. And I couldn't figure out how to argue with him, even though I knew I should.

Wholesoul isn't everything it's cracked up to be.

I knew what Lance was thinking, but that didn't mean I agreed with him. And sensing his feelings didn't mean I shared them.

You'd think two people who could read each other's minds would be of one mind. Lance and me? Not so much.

It would be a long ride back to Cherry Glen.

Chapter 2

The problem with infinite magical power is, it doesn't exist. And the problem with limited magical power? It's usually more trouble than it's worth. I'd tapped my power more in the past three weeks than the rest of my life put together, and what had it gotten me? I was in more danger now than I'd ever been.

Okay, maybe there wasn't a direct correlation. But a case could be made.

And now, the closer we got to Cherry Glen, the more nervous I grew. I couldn't shake the feeling that we were heading into a trap. But I didn't want to stop, because I was also worried about Nonny. She's in Cherry Glen, and she's the only family I've got. Maybe she never officially adopted me, but she may as well have. Which makes her a very tempting target, no doubt, for anyone who might be interested in hurting me.

And Nonny is totally clueless about what's going on. She's never even heard of spellspinners. This makes her a sitting duck. Every time I thought about it I felt my blood pressure climb, and yet I couldn't stop thinking about it. So I clung to Lance as we roared through the night and fretted like a helicopter parent on prom night.

When we reached the outskirts of Pikesville, about ten miles north of Cherry Glen, Lance decided he'd had enough of the restless clamor going on in my brain. He pulled into a deserted parking lot behind a hardware store and killed the engine. The sudden silence made my ears ring.

"Talk to me."

"Okay. Gladly." I got off the motorcycle, with some difficulty, and started pacing. I didn't look at Lance yet. I didn't dare. Looking at Lance messes with my head, and I needed to gather my wits. "Three things: I'm worried about

Nonny, I feel like the Council is probably way ahead of us. And I'm freaking out because we have no plan."

"Our plan is to get your power stone. They took mine. We need yours."

"Yeah, but the Council will guess we're heading for Cherry Glen. They're not stupid. They know that's where I would go, at least. I bet they're already there, waiting for us."

"Not all of them. Only those who can skatch there. You know skatching is limited to places you've already been. Very few spellspinners have been to Cherry Glen. Just Rune, Amber…"

"I don't need a list. I need to know how we can get past them." Now I looked at him. "The ones who can be there, will be there. Even if there's only six, we're outnumbered three to one. And if you and I get picked up again and whisked back to Spellhaven, we're toast. The last time we saw the Council, they were debating whether to let me live. Now that you've helped me escape, you'll be slated for elimination too."

"Nah." He leaned back and gave me a sly grin. "You're extra. I'm genetically valuable."

He had a point. The Council's main problem with my existence — if I understood the matter — was that I'd popped up out of nowhere. There are only supposed to be 49 spellspinners in the world at any given time, their bloodlines monitored as carefully as prize livestock. My appearance in the world, a 50th spellspinner of unknown parentage, had caused a disturbance in the Force. So to speak.

Lance, on the other hand, was part of the grand design and had already been pre-matched with a mathematically-chosen female spellspinner who wasn't me. And who hated my guts, for obvious reasons.

"Okay," I said. "They'll spare you the death sentence and imprison you instead. You've just had a taste of that. I don't think you liked it any better than I did."

"I didn't." His mouth set in a grim line. "We need your power stone in the worst way."

"Wait. Why? Are we going to *fight* them? That's crazy."

"We don't have to fight them if they take us seriously. But they won't take us seriously if we're weak." His eyes met mine. "Can you skatch yet? Try your bedroom."

I closed my eyes. Tried to pull the power up from the earth—something I shouldn't even have to do, for something as simple as skatching—and transported myself to my bedroom.

I knew before I opened my eyes that it hadn't worked. My bedroom isn't cold and windy, and it doesn't smell of asphalt.

I kicked at the gravel in frustration. "No luck. I wonder what's wrong?"

"You're spellbound. They took my power stone, but they didn't actually bind me—no more than they needed to, to keep me jailed. I think Pearl Doyle put the whammy on you, Zara. She's good."

"Well, how can I break it? My power stone is in Nonny's cedar chest."

"You want a plan? Here's the plan. We get to that cedar chest as quickly and as quietly as we can. We slip in, we get the stone, we slip out. Then we skatch someplace where the Council won't look for us. Even that motel would be better than—"

"No. Wait. Hold it." I shook my head as if to clear it. "You're taking me all this way so I can be home for, like, five minutes?"

"Less than that, if we can manage it."

I stared at him in amazement. "What about Nonny?"

He looked away, but I read the answer in his thoughts. I planted my fists on my hips. "This is not negotiable," I said, and let him feel how upset I was. "Once I get home, I'm staying."

"Zara." I sensed his impatience, but his voice was almost gentle. "Your life there is over. You know it's over. You can't go back. You vanished right in the middle of the Homecoming dance."

"I had nothing to do with that!"

"It doesn't matter who did it. It happened, and it happened in front of sticks. Everybody saw it. You're done with Cherry Glen."

Lance's face blurred as my eyes filled with tears. I dashed them angrily away, furious that I was losing it now, after I'd managed to be so freaking strong through crisis after crisis. Unbelievable.

I fought to get a grip. "You have to let me see Nonny," I said, my voice shaking. "I have to know that she's all right. I've been gone for ages. Anything could have happened. They might have ambushed her, tied her up, hidden her somewhere—she might be hurt. She might be frightened. She might be—" I couldn't say it. *She might be dead.*

Lance leaned toward me, his green eyes glowing, cat-like, in the dim blue wash from the streetlight. "Zara Norland," he said softly. "You're forgetting something."

I stared at him for a moment, uncomprehending. Then I saw the images in his brain and felt my jaw drop. He was right. I'd completely forgotten. Probably because it felt like it happened when dinosaurs walked the earth, but really it had only been a few weeks.

Lance and I had joined forces about a month ago to spin a defensive spell, building a barrier that spellspinners could not cross. It placed my house—Nonny's house, technically—inside a kind of unbreakable snowglobe of protection. Which is great, if you want to keep hostile spellspinners from attacking. Not so great if you happen to also be a spellspinner yourself.

The shield was so effective, even Lance and I could only get past it by skatching. And at the moment, I couldn't skatch.

But right now I didn't care if the shield kept me out, as long as it kept the others out too.

"Do you think it's still there?" I asked.

Lance shrugged. "I don't know why it wouldn't be."

"Um." Worry gnawed at me again. I crossed my arms over my chest and shivered. "Maybe because I had a hand in building it. Everything I do comes undone, remember?"

"Not everything. Not anymore. You're getting stronger all the time."

I rolled my eyes. "Yeah, right. I'm so powerful. I can't even skatch home."

"That's temporary, babe. Maybe by the time we reach the shield, you'll be close enough to your power stone to overcome Pearl's spell."

I tried to smile. "Here's hoping. And don't call me 'babe.'"

"I said 'bae.'"

"No you didn't."

Like it mattered.

If I couldn't break the binding spell, I'd be stuck out in the meadow, banging my fists against an invisible wall, unable to get home. But I could live with that. My getting home wasn't as important as Nonny being safe.

Lance read that thought in my mind but, predictably, didn't agree. He frowned. "It's you I'm worried about. I want to get you somewhere where they can't reach you."

"If the shield still holds," I said, "Nonny's house will be as good a place as any."

"If it holds," he agreed, reluctantly. "And if we can both skatch past it. That's two 'ifs.'"

"Do we need a backup plan?"

Lance's wicked smile gleamed in the darkness. "Get on the bike, babe. Fortune favors the brave."

Lance gets off on danger.

Me? I'm not really into it.

But I got back on the bike. The boy is hard to resist.

There's nothing like the roar of a motorcycle to make you conspicuous in Cherry Glen, especially during the wee hours of the morning. And if spellspinners were watching for us anywhere, they'd be watching the road where Nonny and I live. So we wanted no motorcycle roar, and we wanted to avoid Chapman Road.

Fortunately, I know this little valley like the back of my hand.

We took the long way round, down by Silver Creek, and approached the Chapman property — and the Norland place beyond it — from the back. And then we ditched the bike while still out of earshot. We were about two miles from Nonny's house.

The motorcycle wasn't as heavy as I feared it would be. We dragged it into a thicket of blackberries and scrub oak where the creek bends, right by the Chapman property line. Lance had never been this far past my house, but I knew every bush and tree. "Come on," I whispered. Even out here, where no one would be looking for us, I was too scared to speak out loud. "This way." I started scrambling up the rise, brushing the blackberry dust off my sweats.

"Wait a minute. Is there water in the creek this time of year?"

"Not drinkable. Sorry."

"I don't need to drink it. I just want to look at it."

I paused in the act of pulling a bramble out of my sleeve. Lance was still at the foot of the rise and almost invisible in the darkness. But I saw his sly smile in my mind. And in a flash, I understood why he was asking.

"Lance," I breathed. "You are so smart."

I half-scrambled, half-slid back down the slope toward him. "If there's water, it will be mostly mud. Will that matter?"

"Not much. We should try anyway."

We had our night vision by this time, so it wasn't hard to find the creek. Or what there was of it. The rainy season hadn't begun yet, so there wasn't much to find. "I'm glad it's dark," I muttered. "I bet if we could see this gluck, we wouldn't want to step in it." I was trying not to get my feet wet, in the flimsy canvas slip-ons Lance had bought for me with his ill-gotten gains. And I was failing. "Bleah."

"Stop complaining. There's water here. And it's a safe bet it hasn't been processed in any way."

"That's for sure."

This was important, because — unfortunately — watersight doesn't work once the water has been tampered with. I'd love to be able to gaze into a cup of coffee and astrally project myself to Paris, but that's never gonna happen. Even tap water doesn't cut it, because it's been treated with chloride and fluoride and whatever. Rainwater is nice when you can get it, but creekwater will do in a pinch. And we were in a pinch.

I felt a stab of disquiet when I noticed that my objections to using spellspinner powers were growing dimmer with each passing hour. I added this to the list of things I would think about later. Right now, we were going to pull out every stop to do a little under-the-radar scouting around. And watersight was the best tool we had.

"Where are we going, anyway?"

"Your house. Look out for that rock."

"Ow." Too late. "Can I get to my house through watersight? Even if I can't skatch?"

"Yes. And I'm hoping that once we do, the skatch will be easier. Watersight will take part of us there, so we won't have to skatch our whole selves, if you know what I mean. Just the part of us that's left behind, here at the creek."

"That's brilliant." My admiration was wholly sincere. And I felt the flush of pleasure it gave Lance. So I had to knock him down a peg. "If it doesn't work, I'm going to push you right into this filthy water."

"And if it does work?" His slow smile made my heart go pitty-pat. "I'll expect a suitable reward."

My breath constricted in my throat. "We'll see," I said. But my voice came out in a whisper.

Lance was standing over a puddle. I couldn't really see it, and could barely make out Lance, but I caught the glimmer of starlight reflected in water and saw his hand go out to me.

I took it, and he pulled me to his side.

You know, in times of darkness and danger, it is truly amazing that there is room for wholesoul to blindside you. But there is. And it does.

The linking of our hands kindled wholesoul like lightning ignites a brush fire. For hours I'd been hanging onto him on the back of the motorcycle, trying to ignore the rush it gave me. Although it was difficult, it had, at least, been possible—since I wasn't touching his skin, and we were both concentrating on the journey. But taking his hand in the dark, standing in the muck by the creek, was completely different. I couldn't say why. It just was.

Our eyes met. We stared wordlessly at each other for a long moment, just taking it in as wholesoul roared in our veins and throbbed in our temples, heady as heroin and probably twice as dangerous.

It's the most wonderful feeling in the world, when you meet someone who completes you. Total oneness, total communication. Complete understanding.

But when your other half is someone you don't approve of, the intense feeling of belonging is also frightening. I looked away, gulping for air. "Enough," I whispered. "It's too much."

Lance agreed with me. He didn't like it either.

I mean, we both *like* it — it's impossible not to. But he has his own reasons for wishing he could pull away. His reasons have to do with independence, solitude, and self-reliance. He doesn't want to need anybody. He's not used to caring about, even thinking much about, anyone other than Lance Donovan. Wholesoul makes me important to Lance, and that bothers him.

I wish my own objections were that simple. To me, our wholesoul is a tad worse than an inconvenience. It's a threat to everything and everyone I'd ever known or cared about.

If Lance and I are one, what becomes of my life? I like my life. A lot. And ever since I met Lance, I've been clinging to it with both hands, feeling it slip through my fingers like rope, burning as it goes. Forces I don't understand are dragging me in directions I don't want to go.

So Lance and I are both fighting it, but our reasons are vastly different. As are we.

Another thing to think about later. Right now, there was no time to ponder the intricacies of wholesoul.

I looked down at my feet and tried to make out the puddle. *Do we have to look at the same place?*

More or less. You're overthinking things again.

Hah. In my opinion, I was *under*thinking things.

"Tell me the rules again," I said. "Remember, I've only done this once. If there are other spellspinners around, will they be able to see us?"

"Depends on how powerful they are. But we're going to your house, so there won't be any spellspinners other than you and me. Sticks won't be able to see us at all."

I frowned. "Don't call Nonny a stick."

"Is she a spellspinner?"

"No."

Silence.

I sighed. "Okay. Whatever. She won't be able to see us. *If* she's there, which I sure hope she is. And she also can't hear us if we talk, right?"

"Our voices stay with our bodies. We'll hear each other, because our bodies are standing here next to each other. Nobody at your house will hear us. Anybody walking by here would hear us, though, so I still wouldn't shout or anything. The last thing we need is some stick finding the two of us standing here in the mud, staring at the ground."

I shivered. "Yeah. With our luck, we're trespassing."

His smile was wicked. "Well, most people say something before they shoot. 'Freeze,' or 'What are you kids doing in my creek.'"

"Oh, goodie. I feel much better."

Silent laughter shook his shoulders. "Seriously, Zara. We'll hear anybody who comes by here. So if we're discovered, we just pop back here and deal with it."

"Okay." My nerves were stretched taut as a guitar string. Hope and fear and excitement and dread thrummed through me in equal measure. I was dying to get home. I was terrified of what I would find. Lance's hand touching mine shot tingles up my arm and made it hard to concentrate.

It'll be all right, Zara.

You don't know.

Okay, I don't know. But we have to do this. Come on. You lead, I'll follow. You know this place better than I do.

Knowing I had to lead helped me focus.

I took a deep breath. "Here goes," I whispered. And I sent my mind swirling down into the water, pulling Lance with me.

I'd forgotten how much I hate watersight.

The world tipped sideways. I fell off.

Down and down and down I fell, biting my tongue to keep from screaming. I would have broken the bones in

Lance's hand from grabbing it so tightly, but his hand — and mine — were back in the thicket by the creek. The hand I clutched so desperately had no substance, and my frantic grip inflicted no damage. It also brought no comfort.

We surfaced in the yellow scrub grass behind Nonny's house, just a step or two from the kitchen door. "Oh," I gasped. I bent over and seized my knees, waiting for the planet to right itself. Which was ridiculous, because I couldn't feel my knees. The dizziness did subside, but it probably would have anyway.

The faint gray light of oncoming dawn turned the familiar shapes and sights of home weirdly dreamlike. It was very still. Even the neighbors' rooster wasn't crowing in the distance. A strange, fluttering light ebbed and flickered somewhere in the house. For one terrified second I thought the house was on fire. I leaped to the top of the stoop and walked through the door — literally. Since my body had no substance, I couldn't open it. But I could pass right through the wood and metal, and I did.

The kitchen was darker than it had been outside, but the flickering light was stronger. I heard strange sounds now, as well; the murmur of voices and…violins?? It was coming from the front parlor.

Lance materialized beside me. He could feel my fear and confusion. "Zara, it's a television," he said, in the voice one uses to soothe a panicked child.

I looked at him. He stood beside me, transparent and ghostlike, but still definitely Lance. What he said didn't make sense, however. "At this hour?" I whispered — forgetting that no one could hear us. "Nonny hardly ever watches TV. Why would she be watching something at — " I glanced at the numbers glowing on the coffeemaker. "Five a.m.?"

He shrugged. "Let's go see."

I floated uneasily across the kitchen, through the dining room and into the parlor. Sure enough, the TV was on, with the volume low. An old, black-and-white movie was playing. And there, curled on the sofa with one of her hand-crocheted throws tucked around her, was Nonny. I was so relieved to see her safe and sound, in her own home, with not a mark on her, that tears started in my eyes. "Thank God," I said fervently.

And then I noticed the circles under her eyes. Her hair was unkempt and looked like it hadn't been washed in a while. Her face looked thinner. She was staring at the movie with eyes that obviously didn't see it; they were fixed and glassy, and her haunted expression did not change when the actors on the screen laughed merrily. I turned to Lance again. "I've seen enough," I said. "Let's skatch."

"Not here," he warned me. "You'll scare her."

He was right. The sight of us popping out of thin air might give her a heart attack.

"My room," I said. "Come on. If I can skatch anywhere, it'll be there." I led the way up the stairs and pushed myself through my bedroom wall.

And stopped. If Lance and I had had any substance, we would have collided painfully. He floated on through me, however, and stopped at my side. Together, we stared at my bed.

There was someone in it.

Worse.

The someone was me.

Chapter 3

The window beside my bed — the one that opens onto the porch roof — was uncovered and partially open, just the way I like it. Eerie gray light bathed the room. Straight, silky black hair streamed across my pillows and comforter. I saw the curve of a familiar cheek and the equally-familiar outline of a slim feminine form curled like a cat. One long, pale arm was flung wide; the other hugged the battered teddy I've slept with since I was two.

She was wearing my favorite jammies.

I was so disoriented by the sight, I forgot my body was back at the creek. A strange, low, keening sound — almost a growl — rose in my throat as I ran to the bed and tried to shake the girl awake. My hands went right through her shoulders, disappearing as if I'd plunged them into dark water.

Lance's voice sounded, sharp with authority. "Zara, stop. Get a grip."

"Get a grip?" I gave a breathless laugh, on the verge of hysteria. "I can't even touch her." But she sensed my touch after all; she shivered in her sleep and pulled the comforter higher. I couldn't see her face.

But the raven hair was mine. The pale arm was mine. Even the teddy was mine!

My transparent fingers tugged fruitlessly at the comforter, tried vainly to shove her hair back, and yanked on the pillow. Nothing budged. I pounded my fist in frustration against the bed, feeling nothing but air because I was nothing but air. "Who is she? This makes no *sense.*"

"There will be a logical explanation."

"Well, thank you, Mr. Spock. When will we have that, exactly? In the meantime, excuse me while I have a nervous breakdown."

His ghostly face almost smiled. "See? You're feeling better already."

"Don't let my sarcasm fool you. I'm coming unglued." I remembered that I wasn't bound by corporeal restrictions in my present state, and swam over to the windowsill. Balanced there, I crouched to look into the girl's face. I cast no shadow; the light coming through the window poured right through me. If her face had been visible, I would have seen it. But my cold, cold touch on her shoulder a moment ago had sent her burrowing into the comforter, and I still couldn't see her face. Frustration rose in me like bile.

He felt my intention and shot me a warning. *You're on the windowsill.*

I sheepishly floated back to the rag rug on the floor by my bed. *Guess if I skatched to the windowsill I might fall, huh?*

"Or break the window when you arrived. You're too impulsive." He shook his head, genuinely troubled. "Sometimes I think being raised by sticks has made you more stick than spellspinner."

"Well, let's hope the spellspinner part of me is strong enough to get me here, because I'm going to skatch. Try, anyway."

"It should work this time. Remember, your power stone is just downstairs."

I nodded, still nervous after all my failed attempts over the past couple of days. But then I realized he was right. I could feel the nearness of my power stone, like a fizz in the air, or like a deep hum, a vibration just below my hearing threshold. Having been away from it for so long, I was newly aware of its presence.

Confidence filled me, sweet as birdsong. I didn't even have to try; the skatch rose seamlessly from my intent and *boom,* there I was — all of me — standing on the rag rug in my very own bedroom.

It felt good.

I leaned over that imposter Zara and yanked the covers off her in one smooth move. She came with them, tumbling out of my bed and onto the floor with a satisfying thump.

I tossed the bedclothes aside and pounced, rolling her onto her back and straddling her like a roped calf. She blinked dazedly up at me, bleary with sleep. "Ow," she said faintly.

We stared at each other. Of course she wasn't me. Duh.

But gooseflesh prickled on my arms anyway.

It was like an echo of the day I met Lance. I remember the strangeness, and the thrill, of encountering another spellspinner for the first time...after feeling, all my life, like a space alien who'd somehow fallen off the mothership. Lance was the first person I'd ever met who reminded me of *me*.

And this girl was the second.

She looked an awful lot like I might look if I weren't a spellspinner. She looked like stick-Zara. Her eyes weren't amethyst-purple, they were hazel or something. Her skin wasn't unnaturally pale, like mine, but it was very fair.

For one spooky second, I wondered if she looked enough like me to have fooled Nonny, and that's how she got into my house, my bedroom and my jammies. Then I gave myself a mental shake. A lot of crazy things had happened lately, but that crazy? No.

I gave her my most ferocious scowl. "Who are you?"

The fuzziness of deep sleep was evaporating quickly from her features. I saw her eyes focus and recognition dawn in them. Her eyes — so like mine, but the wrong color — widened in an expression of shock so deep it looked like horror. "Zara," she whispered.

I grabbed her shoulders in a grip that was probably painful. "Guess again," I snapped. "*I'm* Zara. Who are you?"

To my astonishment, her eyes welled with tears. "Zara," she repeated. She sounded like she was about to choke. "Oh, I can't believe it. Zara." Her body moved convulsively beneath mine, with surprising strength, and I suddenly found myself wrapped in a bear hug. Stunned, I permitted it. It seemed the only thing to do. My doppelgänger was *crying*.

She sobbed and gulped and rocked me back and forth. I looked past her shoulder and saw Lance, still a transparent outline, watching the scene with a sort of clinical fascination. I shrugged helplessly and answered his unspoken question. *Your guess is as good as mine.*

His lips moved.

I can't hear you anymore, I reminded him.

He grinned, and sent his thoughts into my brain. *I'm heading out. Going to skatch to the meadow and approach the house on foot.*

I nodded, and watched his ghostly form float through the wall and vanish. Interesting. Whatever was going on here, he clearly thought I was in no danger or he would have stayed. The nutcase weeping into my ugly sweatshirt might be unhinged, but at least Lance thought she wasn't homicidal.

My bedroom door banged open. Nonny stood on the threshold, fiercely brandishing a baseball bat. The next couple of minutes were a blur, during which she dropped the bat and I got away from my evil twin and into Nonny's hug instead. Tears may have been shed at this point by Nonny. Or me. Or both of us. As I say, it was a blur.

Turns out Nonny had heard the thump when the girl in my bed hit the floor, and assumed the worst — since things have been strange around here lately. Hence the baseball bat. Nonny is nothing if not protective.

We established that: (a) both of us were all right, (b) we had been sick with worry about each other, (c) we thought we'd never see each other again, and (d) we were overjoyed to be wrong about that. Then I thought it was time to move on.

I pointed at my doppelgänger. "Who is this?"

A strange silence fell.

"It's Raina, honey," Nonny said at last. Her face had an odd, strained expression. "I think I told you about Raina. My friend from the commune?"

I looked from Nonny to Raina and back again, trying to remember what Nonny had told me. Not much. But the name did sound familiar.

Then I had it. "The girl who disappeared? I thought she was your age."

"A bit younger," said Raina softly. "At the time. Much younger now."

Another silence. Nobody moved.

"Okaaaay," I said. "I think I need a cup of tea. Strong tea. In fact, I may need coffee."

Nonny's eyebrows rose. "You never drink coffee."

"I might make an exception."

We trooped downstairs to the kitchen. Nonny flipped the lights on and bustled around, the very act of tying an apron around her waist visibly relaxing her. "Do you really want coffee?" she asked, beginning to fill the coffeepot.

"I do," said Raina.

"French toast," I said. I knew that would perk her up, and it did. Nonny's face brightened. She looked almost like her old self as she moved into the familiar rhythm of cooking. Which reminded me yet again how different we are.

Really, it was amazing that she had to *tell* me — on my sixteenth birthday — that we aren't related. Nonny is short and square, brown as a nut from working outdoors, efficient and motherly and, well, just as different from me as two people can be. Raina, on the other hand…

Raina was standing beside me, her eyes fixed on me with an almost painful intensity. She was wearing my favorite terrycloth bathrobe, thank you very much, and in full light she looked more like me than ever. She was exactly my height. Her slim hands — so like mine — reached for my shoulders. She turned me to face her. I automatically dropped my eyes, because it makes me tense when people look at my eyes. My smooth, pale skin is unusual enough, but the violet eyes are downright freaky. "Look at me," she said quietly.

Reluctantly, I complied. To refuse would have been cowardly.

Her eyes — sort of a gray-green in the strong overhead light of Nonny's kitchen — searched my features. Now that I got a good look at her, I saw she was a tad older than me. Not a high-schooler. She looked, maybe, college-age. And our features, while eerily similar, were not identical. Not a doppelgänger after all. Of course, if anything, that deepened the mystery. And then she said, "You are a spellspinner."

My jaw slackened.

I'd never heard that word spoken by any stick other than my best friend, Meg, and Meg only knew it because I told her. Foolishly, according to Lance, but that seemed beside the point now. Evidently sticks knew about us after all. At least Raina did.

My eyes cut nervously toward Nonny. She was rummaging in the refrigerator, humming, and clearly hadn't heard.

"Fear not, little one," said Raina — although I wasn't any littler than she was. "The time for secrets is past."

Right on cue, the screen door squeaked and a knock sounded on the kitchen door. Nonny froze in her tracks, halfway between the refrigerator and the stove. "It's all right," I said. "I'll get it."

Letting Lance in was a relief. My brain paused for half a second to register the irony of this — since the last time he was in our kitchen, *relief* was probably the opposite of what I'd felt. Strange to think of Lance Donovan as an ally. He picked up some of what I was thinking and his lips curved in a sly half-smile. I punched his arm and growled. His smile widened into a grin.

Oops. Neither of us had spoken.

"Come on in, Lance," I said, possibly a bit too loudly. "Nonny's making French toast."

"Sounds great," he said. "How are you, Ms. Norland?"

Nonny hadn't moved. Her kind, merry face did not easily convey hostility, but I recognized it even so. She had never liked Lance. And now she had every reason to like him even less. After all, his appearance in Cherry Glen coincided with her comfortable world dissolving into chaos. From her perspective, Lance was nothing but bad news — and brought nothing but bad news.

I spoke quickly, before Nonny had a chance to order him out of her house. "Lance saved my life," I said. "And he brought me home. I wouldn't have made it without him."

Raina had seated herself at the kitchen table. She studied Lance with nearly the same intensity she had studied me. "Another spellspinner," she said.

Lance's head whipped around to stare at her. He's way too cool to jump or anything, but Raina's quiet voice had shocked him to the core.

"Welcome to my world," I muttered. "It gets weirder every minute."

Nonny started moving again. She wasn't happy, but I took her return to French toast-making as a good sign. "Set the table, Zara," she said. "Lance may as well stay for breakfast. Then we'll see."

I waved Lance toward the table. "Raina, this is Lance Donovan," I said. "Lance, this is Raina. She's, um…" My voice trailed off as I struggled to finish the sentence without saying, *the girl you saw in my bed.* I was reaching for, maybe, *an old friend of Nonny's* or something like that, when Raina finished the sentence for me.

"I'm Zara's mother," she said. And reached matter-of-factly to shake Lance's hand.

Chapter 4

It was good that I hadn't picked up the plates yet. I would have dropped them for sure. I stood in the middle of the kitchen, thunderstruck. I couldn't move. I couldn't even breathe.

Meanwhile, Lance reached automatically to shake Raina's hand. He'd already recovered his cool; you can't keep that boy off-balance for long. "Well, well," he said calmly. "This is a surprise."

Lance has a gift for understatement.

My life was flashing before my eyes, the way they say it does when you get hit by a truck. Me, the baby left at the gates of a commune, wrapped in an embroidered blanket edged with sparkling stones.

I saw my childhood in the commune with Nonny...Nonny hustling us out of there in the dark, as if we were running from the mob, and moving us here...secrets, secrets, secrets...a little girl with strange powers, and a guardian desperate to suppress them, praying she'd outgrow them. And overarching everything, the huge LIE my life was built on, that Nonny was my aunt. That my father was unknown, but my mother had been Nonny's younger sister, who died the summer I was born...a lie unmasked last summer, when Lance arrived and showed me what I was.

What I was, but not who I was.

Even once I knew I was a spellspinner, my origins remained a mystery. According to Lance—and even the Council, who supposedly knew everything—my existence was impossible. There had been no spellspinner death, no break in the ranks, that tallied with my birth.

I was the fiftieth spellspinner—a creature that should not exist.

And here sat another creature who should not exist: A way-too-young woman with my hair and my build, a *stick,* of all things, who said she was my mother. But sticks don't give birth to spellspinners. And girls in their twenties don't have teenaged daughters.

The room was dissolving into black dots. This reminded me that I hadn't taken a breath for a while. I gulped in air and clutched a chairback, my knuckles going white where I gripped it. It's a miracle the wood didn't snap.

I felt an arm go around my waist. "Sit down, Zara," said Nonny. "I'll set the table."

"Allow me," said Lance, heading for the cupboards.

I slipped into the chair across from Raina, still unable to speak. Raina's eyes never left my face. Her expression was odd, I thought. Sad. Almost compassionate.

"You cannot take it in," she said. "Believe me, I know. At first I thought I might die. Then I wondered if I already had. But no. It is life itself that is strange and unpredictable."

Her words slid right past me. "You're my mother," I said. My voice sounded hoarse. "Really?"

"Really." She looked down at her hands. Emotion flitted briefly across her features, then was gone. "I missed your childhood. That wasn't supposed to happen."

She sure didn't seem worked up about it. Anger licked through me, hot and primitive. "Where were you?"

"Far away," she whispered. The gray-green eyes met mine. "And long ago."

Was it shock that kept me from feeling surprised by this? Or had I known, somehow, already?

Because I wasn't surprised. At all.

"Time travel," I said numbly.

She nodded.

"That's not possible," said Lance. He was at the silverware drawer, frowning into it as if the spoons displeased him. I uttered a short bark of mirthless laughter. His expression did not change. The irony of a spellspinner calling something 'impossible' was lost on him.

"It's impossible for us," I told him. "It might be possible for her. I had a big conversation with Rune about this."

"You did, huh?" He strolled over and started placing forks and knives. "How did the subject come up, exactly?"

Don't be snarky. "He's supposed to have all this arcane knowledge. So I asked him. I wanted to know if spellspinners could travel through time." My eyes cut toward Nonny again. It felt odd, to say the least, to say 'spellspinner' right in front of a couple of sticks. "Rune told me we can't. But the reason why we can't is connected to the reason why we can't get a tan."

"Yeah? This ought to be good." He slid into the chair next to mine.

I sighed. "You know this stuff better than I do. Some of the natural planetary properties don't affect us the way they affect sti— other people. Rune says the planet has wormholes, but spellspinners walk right through them. We don't get sucked in. When a sti—um, that is, when other people—most people—step into a wormhole, they end up somewhere else. Some*when* else."

"Both," said Raina softly. "In my case. And I don't mind if you call me a stick."

I was startled when Nonny slammed a plate of French toast down in front of me. She hadn't said a word. She gave everyone a full plate, then marched back for the coffee and syrup. Lance and I exchanged a glance. Then I looked at Raina. "It upsets her," Raina explained.

"I bet," I murmured. This must be awful for Nonny. She had been so uncomfortable with my powers, feeble as they were in early childhood, that I'd tried for years to hide them.

Nonny poured coffee in silence, then joined us. Her expression was strained. She looked pale and tired. "I'm too old for this stuff," she said. "Sorry. I'm not handling it well."

"Handling what well?" I asked.

"This." She waved her hand vaguely, incorporating Lance and Raina in the circle of things she wasn't handling well. "All this woo-woo heebie-jeebie stuff."

"Reality — " Raina began, but Nonny shook her head.

"Makes it worse when you call it reality. Leave me be. You just go on and talk amongst yourselves."

Lance looked thoughtful. "I'd be interested to know," he said politely, "what this looks like from your perspective. A normal person's perspective. What do you think happened at the Homecoming dance, for example? Is there an explanation that doesn't involve anything, um, heebie-jeebie?"

"How would I know?" Nonny buttered her French toast with little stabbing motions. I had rarely seen her so edgy. "I wasn't there. They say a bunch of people showed up at the dance. Strangers. Nobody invited them, and nobody can find them after the fact. All hell broke loose, several people were injured, and my little girl vanished. Along with all the strangers. And you." She pointed her knife at Lance. "I haven't said so to the police, because I have no proof, but it's my belief those weirdos were with you. You're behind this whole thing, somehow. I'd stake my life on it."

"Don't," said Lance quietly. "Because you'd lose."

"No she wouldn't," I said. "They *were* with you."

"It's complicated," he said, and dug into his French toast.

Nonny abruptly shifted her focus to me. "By the way, young lady, the police have your purse and your phone."

"The *police?* Why?"

"Confiscated as evidence."

I rolled my eyes. "Fat lot of good it'll do them. How do I get my phone back?"

"You don't," said Lance. "We're not going near the police. They can't help us anyway."

"No, they can't," said Raina. "But I can."

We all stared at Raina. She set her fork down neatly beside her plate and folded her hands. "I don't know where you two have been, any more than Helga does." She jerked her head to indicate Nonny, since she was the only one at the table who called Nonny 'Helga.' "But if I were to guess, I'd guess Spellhaven."

A chill ran down my spine and Lance shivered. We're so connected, I don't know whether the chill started as mine or his. But to hear a stick speak of Spellhaven, the secret refuge of our race, rang all sorts of primitive alarms along both our nerves.

She didn't seem to notice. "I came back because I didn't know whether Zara was a stick or a spellspinner. I knew if she were a spellspinner, there'd be trouble sooner or later. Thing is, I thought I was coming back to get my baby. I didn't realize she'd be all grown up — or nearly — by the time I got here. And that the trouble would have already begun. When Helga told me what happened at the Homecoming dance — "

"Wait. Wait." I held up my hand. "Start at the beginning."

Raina looked lost for a moment. "The beginning?"

I took a deep breath and closed my eyes. Then opened them.

"Once upon a time there was a girl named Raina," I said. "She lived in a commune with a bunch of other New Age types and grew organic vegetables. Then, one day, she…?"

"Ah." Raina's expression softened as she looked inward, recalling that day. "She had a big fight with her mother and went for a walk in the woods to cool down. A long walk. And just as she was about to turn back and start home, she saw something glitter in the light at the bottom of a ravine. A shaft of sunlight just happened to be falling right on it, whatever it was, and it caught the light and sparkled.

She thought, 'What on earth is that?' and went down the side of the ravine to see. But when she reached the foot of the cliff, she tripped over a root and fell forward. It shouldn't have been a bad fall, there in the bracken, but somehow she kept falling and falling and falling..." Raina's voice trailed off and she closed her eyes. "I landed in a field of flax. It was June, and the field was in bloom. Brilliant, beautiful blue flowers all around me, and a cloudless sky overhead...blue, blue, blue. As blue as the eyes of the man bending over me."

Her voice had taken on a hypnotic, almost sing-song quality, but she suddenly fell silent. Her eyes flew open and she glanced at the faces around the table. "I sound like an idiot."

Nonny smiled a little. "You sound like a Celtic tale-teller," she said. "Your granny used to sound like that, as I recall. Once she got going."

"I'll try to wrap it up a little faster than granny would," said Raina. "You don't need to know the painful truth anyhow—how long it took me to accept what had happened, how hard it was to understand the people around me, even though, supposedly, we were all speaking English." She shook her head, her expression wry. "It was not pleasant. And I behaved very badly. So we'll skip ahead, if you don't mind."

"Where were you?" I asked.

"Wiltshire, actually," she replied, sounding perfectly matter-of-fact.

"England," said Nonny flatly. "You fell into England."

"I know this is hard for you, Helga—"

"Not at all." Nonny folded her arms across her chest, glaring at Raina. "It's a great story. Very entertaining. Go on."

Raina looked at Lance and me, seeming apologetic. "It gets crazier," she said. "I hadn't just traveled through space, I'd traveled through time as well. I landed in the summer of 1699."

Nonny abruptly rose and headed for the coffeepot. Raina watched her with a worried, slightly guilty expression.

"She'll be okay," I said. "This might even be good for her."

"She thinks I'm conning her," said Raina sadly. "Although she can't figure out why I'd want to, or exactly how I'm doing it. Poor Helga. She's sure this is some kind of hoax."

"But it isn't," said Lance. "So she'll catch up eventually. You just told us you had a hard time believing it too."

Raina looked thoughtful. "That I did. I surely did."

"What about the people around you?" I asked. "In 1699. You were, like, all modern and stuff. Didn't they think you were a witch?"

Nonny poured more coffee into her cup and Raina's, then silently rejoined us. Raina glanced at her, then ducked her chin in a gesture so familiar to me that gooseflesh prickled my arms again. Her raven hair, so like mine, slid down across the side of her face like a curtain, shielding her from Nonny's scrutiny. It was something I did on a daily basis—no, make that an hourly basis—at school, to hide from prying eyes. "They did not harm me," she said softly. "Partly because I was not the first stranger to arrive in that village. It had happened before, from time to time. And partly because I did not stay, once my…oddness…became dangerous. And partly because I had powerful protection."

"The man with the blue eyes," said Lance. "Who found you in the field."

Raina's eyes widened as she looked at Lance. "You're quick," she said. "Yes. He was a spellspinner."

"Why did he protect you?" I asked.

Her lips curved in a strange little smile. "First, from compassion," she said. "And then amusement. I amused him. And eventually he protected me out of love."

"Love?" My hands gripped the edge of the table. "Was he my father?"

Raina reached across to cover my hands with her own. "Yes, Zara," she said. Her voice was full of tenderness. "And a finer man never walked the earth."

I didn't care about that. The details of his character mattered to Raina, not to me. My heart was pounding because I had answers, *answers,* for the first time—answers to questions that had haunted me for ages. Later, I would be glad to know he was a fine man. For now, it was enough to know that he was a spellspinner.

And that my instincts had been right.

My instincts—and Lance's.

I glanced at him, sitting motionless beside me, his impossibly green eyes fixed with utter concentration on my face as he struggled to follow the rapid shifts in my emotions. He was aware of everything I felt, but it was hard for him to keep up. Chaotic feelings were foreign to him, and the insecurities I wrestled with were a mystery to Lance. Which is why he had long suspected, as had I, that there was something 'off' about me. Something more than could be accounted for by my upbringing. I was too emotional, too impulsive, too tender-hearted, too conflicted.

Too human.

"There you have it," I said, hardly aware that I was speaking aloud. "I am half spellspinner, half stick. This explains everything."

"It explains a lot," he said. *If it's true.* "Not everything."

My eyebrows lifted. I had caught that little zinger, although Nonny and Raina were oblivious. *You don't believe her?*

Is there any reason why I should?

This floored me. *Why would she lie?*

Lance shrugged. He still didn't believe in time travel. My temper flared.

"Okay," I said. "Cards on the table. I believe this is true because I suspected it. I've suspected it for a while. I'm not a stick; that's obvious. Normal people can't do what I do. But I'm not normal for a spellspinner either. I'm different. I don't belong with either set. There had to be an explanation. And there were a few clues sewn on my baby blanket—" I stopped. Looked at Raina. "You embroidered that blanket, didn't you?"

She smiled. "Sheared the sheep, spun the cloth, set the stones, embroidered the figures." She shot an amused look at Nonny. "All that organic farming and weaving I did at the commune came in handy, once I landed in the seventeenth century."

Nonny flinched. She obviously hated the time-travel idea even more than Lance did. "The blanket had 'Zara' embroidered on it. But other than her name, it was just decoration, we thought."

I shook my head. "It meant something. It was a warrior in armor and a twentieth-century woman, reaching to each other past the stars. And my…" my throat closed against speaking the words *power stone* aloud. "A special amethyst," I said. "There was a special amethyst sewn in next to my name."

Nonny chuckled. "It's not real, honey."

Raina and I spoke at the same time. "It's real."

We looked at each other. "You put that…stone there for me," I whispered. "You knew what it was."

She nodded. "I thought you'd be a stick, honestly. But I knew that if I were wrong, and you were spellspinner born, you'd need it. As for the clues—I didn't think of the decoration as clues." Humor lit her eyes for a moment. "Had I realized the blanket was needed for that, I'd have made the message plainer. I never dreamed I was dropping out of

Zara's life for years on end. I embroidered it to…I don't know…reflect my story. Illustrate how Zara came to be. And, of course, I had a sense that the blanket shouldn't be plain. It had to be a special blanket because of what it held."

"I'd like to see that blanket," said Lance.

Raina's smile turned cool. "I'll bet you would. It's chock full of power stones."

Lance's mind went blank with shock. It was interesting to feel such a strong reaction coming from unflappable Lance. I patted his knee. "Don't worry," I said, and quoted Raina. "The time for secrets is past."

He stared at me. "The time for secrets is never past. Remember who you are."

"Remember? I'm just now finding out." I turned my attention back to Raina. "So you worked on the blanket while you were pregnant, then brought it forward in time when you had me. Did you come through the wormhole pregnant? It seems risky."

"Not as risky as birthing a child in 1704. Or so I thought. No way was I going to have my baby in 1704. I had already known one woman who hemorrhaged and another who died of childbed fever. Not a pleasant way to go." Raina shuddered. "I wanted to have modern medicine at hand when I gave birth. I was afraid. So as I neared my time, Zach brought me back to Wiltshire —"

"Brought you back?" I said.

"Zach?" said Lance.

She paused, then smiled apologetically. "I skipped a few things. Zachariah is my husband. The man who found me, and protected me. He took me back to his home in Ireland and married me there. That's where we were living — or I was — and a lonely spot it was, with Zach oft away. There were wars between the spellspinners in those days." She looked at me. "Your father is a great leader," she said softly. "And a wise one. You've a proud legacy, Zara.

He brought peace to his people, though 'twas a hard-won peace, and many died—"

Lance sat bolt upright. "Zachariah Wilder?" He stared first at Raina, then at me, then at Raina again. "Zara's father is *Zachariah Wilder?*"

Pride flashed in Raina's eyes. "So his name is known today. And that's as it should be. Yes."

"It's not known to me," muttered Nonny. She gulped the last of her coffee and rose from the table. "Excuse me. This is getting to be a bit much."

Lance rose as Nonny did. The boy's manners are so good, they're practically Victorian. Nonny seemed startled by it, but I know she's a sucker for stuff like that. I hoped she would remember that he set the table, too. She almost smiled at him. "Sit down, Lance," she said. "You're needed. I'm not part of this pow-wow."

"You should be," I said uneasily. I didn't like to leave Nonny out, especially since it's her own home. But she shook her head and moved away, beginning to tidy the kitchen. The three of us looked at each other as Lance sat back down.

"She'll be all right," I said. "Whenever there's a crisis, Nonny cooks and cleans. It's like therapy to her. Connects her to normalcy, she says."

Nonny called over her shoulder. "I can hear you, you know."

"Good." I pointed at Raina with my fork. "Go ahead."

So Lance and I ate and listened, and Nonny tidied up and listened. Lance had definitely heard of Zachariah Wilder. So had I, I soon realized. My father was the guy Rune had told me about, when he was schooling me on spellspinner history—the guy who was such a powerful warrior, and such a great leader, that he managed to end the spellspinner wars. Single-handedly, pretty much.

As Raina told it, when she arrived in the British Isles at the end of the seventeenth century, spellspinners were everywhere. Scattered, and living apart from each other — as they still do — but there were hundreds of them in the world, not just forty-nine. Our power dilutes when there are too many of us, so spellspinners in that day were more numerous, but less powerful. And a few of them got the bright idea that if they formed an alliance and ganged up on the other spellspinners, they could eliminate a few rivals and grow more powerful.

At first, it worked. But alliances shifted and broke as one turned against another and nobody knew whom to trust. Spellspinners are a suspicious lot, and for good reason. As they fell, one by one, those who were left grew stronger — and more dangerous.

So there were wars. All of this was happening in secret, far from the eyes of normal people. When it reached its deadly peak, however, it did spill into the stick world — the spellspinner war caused a ferocious hurricane in 1703. In England, of all unlikely places! Seriously. You can look it up.

It was shortly after the Great Storm that Zachariah Wilder took matters in hand. By this time, the spellspinners had fought themselves nearly to extinction — thus proving, as far as I'm concerned, that spellspinners are just as hopeless as sticks.

My father's brawn and brains saved the day. He had both, and after winning many a battle, he bent his intellect to peacemaking. He acquired all the remaining power stones. All the power stones! This is a feat that boggles the mind. Some were stolen, some were taken by force of arms, some were claimed as forfeit — bargaining chips, in the sense of, "give me your stone and I'll let you live." Then he gathered the spellspinners together for a council. Not a council of war, but a council of government. And a pact was made:

Be with us or against us. All who do not join must die.

Those who band together loyal shall secure the peace thereby.

There were some who refused to join, but without their power stones, their rebellion was easily overcome. In the end, forty-nine were left.

Forty-nine seemed a lucky number: seven times seven. The gestation period for spellspinner babies is seven months instead of nine. It seemed preordained. And spellspinners are always born on the seventh day of the seventh month, which is why Lance and I have the same birthday, July 7th.

"As to the birthdays, that wasn't always so," Raina told us. "Rules were set up at the first Council, to reinforce the pact and give structure to spellspinner society. Once the rules were set, spells were spun to bind them in place. They thought it was lucky to build everything around the number seven." She shrugged. "Perhaps it was, since the structure has survived three hundred years."

"What was the structure?" I asked.

"Seven were elected to the governing Council, and everyone agreed to obey the Council. The more they kept faith only with each other, the safer the spellspinners would be. From that day forward, the blood lines would be monitored and reproduction would be carefully restricted. It was to everyone's benefit to keep the numbers small; they all saw that. 'Twas likewise agreed that with only forty-nine left, diluting the race must be forbidden. So no more mating by choice would be allowed, and no reproducing with sticks. It was the price of peace. Only when one of the forty-nine died would reproduction occur, and only by a couple chosen by the Council, taking the bloodlines into consideration."

"I don't fit in the plan," I said. "Awkward."

"Very." Raina's expression was somber. "By the time the rules were forged, I was heavy with child. You were conceived before the rule was thought of. But still, Zach deemed it fortunate that I wanted to return to my own century to birth you."

"Just in case," said Lance grimly.

Raina nodded. "Just in case. Peace we had, but yet a fragile one. We did not care to begin by asking the Council to bend the rules for us. Even for us." She sighed. "I like to think they would have. Zach sat at the head of the Council, after all."

"So was I, or was I not, born on July 7th?" I asked.

She looked surprised. "You were. And I thought you arrived early, although I wasn't sure. It's difficult to know how far along you are, without ultrasound and all that." A faint laugh shook her. "In retrospect, I should have known you were spellspinner born. I suppose I wanted to spare you that, so I comforted myself by thinking it unlikely."

Lance frowned. "Spare her? That's an odd way to put it."

She looked amused. "Is it a great thing, then, to be a spellspinner? I suppose it must seem so, to you. Forgive me. I have seen only the darkest side of your people." Then her face softened. "Except for Zach. Were you all like Zach, I could rejoice to have a spellspinner child."

"Ahem," I said drily. "Of all the spellspinner children you might have had, you did have Zach's, you know."

"Well, that's true. And you have a look of him."

"Do I? I thought I was a dead ringer for you."

She smiled, her eyes scanning my features. "You have his expression. A certain something about the set of your jaw. There is a strength about your face that my face lacks."

Lance looked critically at me. "She's right," he said.

I rolled my eyes, uncomfortable with all this scrutiny. "All right. Whatever. So you came forward in time and had me in a nice, clean hospital. Then you dumped me at the commune—"

Raina winced and made a faint sound of protest, but I continued. Her abandonment had left a bruise on my soul. High time she knew it.

" — and went back to Zach. Is that about right?"

She bit her lip. "Times were unsettled. He needed me."

"And I didn't? How old was I? A week?"

Lance's fingers, cool and strong, closed around my hand beneath the table. Comfort flowed from his hand into mine, and the painful constriction that had begun in my throat eased. *Thank you*, I sent him. It wasn't easy.

Raina looked troubled. "I didn't mean to stay away. I thought I could control it. I thought you'd be at the commune maybe just a day, or a few hours even, waiting for me. I intended to come back and stay with you. As soon as you were old enough — five or six, maybe — that's when I thought I'd take you back to your father's time." She sighed. "Which, if you'd been a stick, would have raised no objection."

"Well, that's just great." I was really mad now. "You were going to take me to the crummy, stinking century you couldn't stand to have a baby in. Thanks a lot."

"It's beautiful there," she offered. Feebly, I thought. "One century is much like another, really. Human life is full of joy and sorrow, trials and triumphs, no matter when you're living it. Only the details change. And your father being a spellspinner, he couldn't come here, to our time. So I thought I'd take you to his."

"But I'm a spellspinner too!"

"I know that now," she said patiently.

"You knew it then," said Lance. His eyes glittered like ice. "Zara has a power stone."

Raina blushed. "Yes. As it happens." She was looking down at her hands now, avoiding our eyes.

"Wait," I said. "What?"

Lance's gaze remained fixed on Raina, as if she were a snake that might suddenly strike. "Power stones are chosen by the father and worn by the mother. In order for you to have a power stone, your mother had to be wearing the stone when you were conceived and all through her pregnancy. It grows in power as you grow. Wilder knew that, even if she didn't."

"Yes, but I wasn't *sure*," said Raina. "It seemed…it seemed so unlikely. That I would have a spellspinner child."

Lance's lips thinned. "So it was a complete coincidence that Zara had a power stone, and that it was hidden in a baby blanket full of other power stones."

"Well, no, not a coincidence." She lifted her head again, looking first at Lance and then at me. "It was a precaution. I had an amethyst ring. Zach gave it to me, to mark the day we promised to wed. I wore it always; it never left my hand. After Zara was born, I embroidered her name on the blanket, then took the stone out of my ring and sewed it beside her name. I knew that if…*if*…she were a spellspinner, it would become her power stone. It gave me a pang to ruin the ring and leave the stone behind, because I supposed it was a useless gesture. But I couldn't bear to leave her without something of mine. Something from Zach. In case things went wrong…not that I believed they would…" Her voice trailed off.

"Sounds to me like you didn't think it through." *Impulsive,* he sent me. *Typical stick.*

Impulsive, I agreed. *Like me.*

"'Struth, I did not. Planning to return for you was foolish, and I should have known that. Mayhap I did know it, deep in my heart." Her fingers twisted together. "I tried to come forward to have you in 1990. I missed. That should have warned me. And when I went back to Zach, I missed again. I tried to return to 1704 but could get no closer than 1709. Zach had given up waiting for me. He'd left Wiltshire and returned to his life in Ireland. It took months to find him." She paused, remembering, then shook her head. "Well. That's past. The main thing I need you to know — the reason why I came back for you — well, as I say, I thought you'd be a stick, spellspinners being the rarity that they are. But I couldn't be sure. And if you were a spellspinner, I knew there'd be danger. Because even while I was here, having you, the rules of the Council tightened. A stick child, the spellspinners would let pass — I could have brought you back; we might have been able to hide you if necessary, back in that day. But a spellspinner child...for a spellspinner born of a stick, the rule is death. Or so it was in 1709." She looked at Lance. "Is it still the rule?"

He nodded. "In fact, if a spellspinner mates with a stick it doesn't matter whether the kid is a spellspinner or not. They don't wait for the powers to manifest. The rule is death, period. They take no chances."

Raina's shoulders sagged. "I feared as much." She sighed. "I'm glad Zach's Council survived the test of time. But of course that means the laws have held, as well. When Helga told me what happened at the dance — I have to tell you, I didn't think you were coming back."

"We didn't think so either," I said. "But Lance found a way." I gave her the outlines of how Lance and I had been held, bound by spells in Spellhaven, until we defied the Council and escaped.

Raina's glance slid from my face to Lance's. She studied him thoughtfully. "Curious," she said at last. "You look a right spellspinner to me."

I frowned. "A what?"

"Sorry. I mean he looks like a real spellspinner, a proper spellspinner. A spellspinner through and through. And — no offense, Lance — but there aren't many spellspinners who would cross the street to help another escape, let alone risk their own lives. Not without something in it for them."

I bristled at her tone. Which amused Lance, because (as he mentally reminded me), I had said much the same thing about him. More than once. "I like Zara," he said mildly.

Raina gave a snort that might have been laughter. "I see."

"We're not out of danger," I reminded them. "I'm sure Lance will have plenty of opportunities to abandon me if he wants to." *Like you did*, I wanted to say—but didn't.

"I won't want to," said Lance. "But if I might bring us back to the start of this highly interesting conversation—"

"Please do."

His apple-green eyes met Raina's levelly. "You said you could help us."

She looked nervous. "I think I can."

"Don't hedge." Lance's voice took on a steely quality that would have had me shaking in my shoes, if I were Raina. "You sounded quite definite about it, twenty minutes ago."

She spread her hands, palm up, in a gesture of helplessness. "I can try. If there is some way for me to meet with the Council—"

I gave a snort of mirthless laughter. "You think they'll expose themselves like that? Meet with a stick?"

"There must be a way. We'll think of a way. Because I am your only chance. I alone can prove to them that Zara's birth did not break spellspinner law."

Lance frowned. "But it did."

She shook her head. "It couldn't have. Because the laws did not exist when she was conceived. In lawful wedlock, if that matters to anyone."

"It won't," Lance said.

"But the other might," I said. "You can't break a law that isn't on the books. If my parents didn't break any laws..." Hope was beginning to stir. "It's outrageous anyway, to punish me for being born. Rune thought so, and I'm sure others did too."

"Rune thought so, but Rune's not impartial. He likes you. Most of them sided with Amber, and Amber's after your blood."

"Amber's not impartial either," I shot back. "She's counting on having a baby with you in a couple of years. If I'm around that's not gonna happen, and she knows it."

"Zara." I felt the sting of Lance's exasperation. "Amber's not going against the Council. If the Council says you live, you live. Rune's not going against the Council. If the Council says you die, you die. And if they say Amber and I are producing the next spellspinner, we are. You and I can try to change their minds about that, but—"

"But we might not succeed. You don't need to say it." I took a deep, shaky breath. "Just like I don't need to say she's having your baby over my dead body. Because we both know that's on the menu of options too. High on the list, in fact. My dead body."

"That's not funny."

"I'm not laughing."

We had forgotten Raina in the heat of our argument. She cleared her throat to get our attention, and we both jumped like startled fawns.

"I am not following your discussion very well," she said. "But if the spellspinners are breaking into factions, some for you and some against, that's not good news."

I was still upset, so I rounded on her. "You'd rather they all wanted me dead?"

"I would rather they be united, whatever the opinion. Then if we change one mind, we change them all."

"They're not the Borg," I snapped. I didn't care if she understood me or not. "You'll have to convince each one."

"Not quite," said Lance. "She only has to convince the Council."

I threw my hands in the air. "Great. Easy peasy. Now tell me how we get her to Spellhaven."

"We can't. We'll have to get word to them, somehow, to meet us on neutral ground. But how?"

The three of us frowned, considering the problem.

We'd all forgotten about Nonny. Now she spoke. "Woo-woo," she said, wiggling her fingers. "Heebie-jeebie. Pick up a phone."

I do love Nonny.

Chapter 5

I left Lance and Raina to work out our plan. It would start with calling Rune, since he was well-respected, had made a lifelong study of spellspinner lore, was Lance's uncle, and — most importantly — was the closest thing I had to a friend among the forty-eight spellspinners not currently under Nonny's roof. Meanwhile, Nonny was exhausted but couldn't bear to let me out of her sight. So I put her to bed and lay on the quilt beside her, to keep her company while she napped.

With the curtains drawn against the morning, Nonny's bedroom was dim and comforting. I loved the smell of it; the lavender and herbs she kept in potpourri jars, her hand-dipped candles, fragrant with sandalwood even when unlit, mingling with the scent of whatever it was she rubbed on her antique furniture. Her room held mostly original pieces from when the house was built, solid wood, beautiful and heavy and deceptively plain. My eyes traveled around the room, resting on the crocheted pillows, hand-knitted throws, and other marks of Nonny's competent, craftsy domesticity.

Then I pictured the baby blanket Raina had embroidered…and grinned to myself. If Nonny had made that thing, it would have been a work of art, and we wouldn't have had to guess what the figures represented.

Like mother, like daughter. Raina and I lacked the needlework gene.

Nonny, eyes closed, reached over and patted my hand. "So glad you're home, honey," she whispered.

"Me too. Go to sleep."

"You're safe here. I won't let them get you."

"Ditto."

Her forehead wrinkled in puzzlement. "Ditto?"

"I won't let them get you, either. Go to sleep."

I smiled, picturing Nonny fending off creatures of power with a baseball bat. Good old Nonny. Who knows? Maybe it would work. Maybe her courage would warm their hearts, and they'd cut her some slack out of respect.

Yeah, right. My smile faded. Good luck warming the cold, cold hearts of spellspinners.

Nonny was right, though, that we were safe in her home—although she didn't know about the shield Lance and I had built. It must still be holding, or the place would be besieged with our kind by now. I wondered how many spellspinners were in Cherry Glen this very minute. I wondered how many more were on their way. I wondered if they knew Lance and I were already here. And then I fell asleep.

Lance's voice in my head awakened me. *Need you in the kitchen.* I rolled carefully away from Nonny and slipped out without waking her. "What's up?" I said, strolling in from the hallway. I was wide awake and feeling pretty chipper, now that nothing horrible had happened for several hours. "Did you guys come up with a foolproof plan?"

Lance and Raina looked at each other. Raina said "yes" and Lance said "no" at the same time.

"Great," I said. "Just what I hoped to hear."

Raina said, "Lance was able to reach his uncle— Rune, is it? And he agreed to meet with me."

I looked from Raina to Lance and back again. Their expressions were grim. "Sounds perfect. So? What's wrong with it? Because something obviously is."

Raina spoke first. "He wants you and Lance to come with me. He won't see me alone."

Lance frowned. "That's not what bothers me. We wouldn't have let you go alone anyway. Besides, spellspinners prefer to meet face to face. I could have said anything on the phone, and so could Rune. Face to face, it's almost impossible for one spellspinner to lie to another."

"We can sense each other's thoughts, you know," I told Raina. "Or at least pick up what the other spellspinner is feeling."

Or, in the case of Lance and me, conduct entire conversations. But I wasn't going to say that aloud.

Raina looked impressed. "Only the most powerful of your kind could do that in my day. Ah—Zach's day, I mean. So keeping your numbers to forty-nine apparently does make spellspinners more powerful."

"Good," I said. "I'd hate to have them go to all the trouble of killing me for nothing."

Lance ignored my lame attempt at humor. "What bothers me," he said, "is that it's too easy. Rune muted the phone for about a minute, so he discussed it with someone—maybe several someones. But not for long. They agreed to it much too quickly. No negotiation at all. And there was something in his voice…" He moved restlessly to the window and stared out at the meadow as if the answer might be walking toward the house. Which I sincerely hoped it wasn't. "I don't know."

"It makes no matter," said Raina. "He agreed to hear me."

I didn't like the uneasy vibe I was picking up from Lance. "But if Lance thinks it's a trap or something—"

"No, she's right." His clear green eyes met mine. "Raina's testimony is the important thing. We have to go. We agreed to meet Rune at the end of Chapman Road, where our shield touches the ground. I doubt if he'll be alone."

I didn't like that.

"I don't like that," I said, so Raina would know my feelings too.

"We'll stay on our side of the shield and they'll stay on theirs."

"It keeps spellspinners out, Lance. It doesn't work on tazers."

He almost smiled. "You're overthinking things again."

He was right, of course, so I reluctantly agreed. Spellspinners have an instinct for lying low. They'd never zap me. Might draw unwanted attention.

I went upstairs to take the braid out of my hair and put on some normal clothing, choosing old jeans and a pale yellow twinset. Sweet but boring. This was not the time to make a statement. I wanted to look bland and harmless. When I came back downstairs, Raina sat alone at the kitchen table. It looked like she was praying, but she lifted her head and smiled at me when I stepped through the door. She was wearing a brown wool dress I had always hated. On her, it looked good.

"You're a pretty girl, Zara."

I shoved my hands in my back pockets, uncomfortable. I wasn't ready to be alone with this woman yet and I sure wasn't ready to hear her compliments. I hadn't decided how I felt about her. "Where's Lance?"

"He went to change his clothes, too."

"Went where?"

"I've no idea."

Movement caught the corner of my eye. Lance had materialized outside the kitchen window—a clever landing spot for skatching, since it was unlikely anyone else would be standing there. A step, a squeak of the screen door, and he was in the kitchen, looking like himself again: heart-stoppingly gorgeous.

I reached automatically for his mind and hit a wall. Not a good sign.

My eyes flicked over him. Leather jacket, jeans, T-shirt. Ray-Bans. Sort of a motorcycle/bad-boy look, and he wore it *so* well. Except that everything looked brand new.

I reached again to examine his thoughts, and again he blocked me. "Nice," I muttered, disgusted.

"Wow," said Raina, smiling. "Your boyfriend's a fox, Zara."

A fox. There's a blast from the past.

"My boyfriend is also a thief," I said. But not loud enough for Raina to hear.

I knew exactly where Lance had obtained his change of clothes. He'd skatched to the not-open-at-this-hour mall and helped himself.

He lifted the Ray-Bans from his face and pinned me with his Kryptonite eyes. *What should I have done, Zara? Skatch back to my room and change there?*

His room. Right. That's where his clothes were, in the rental Lance shared with Rune — or did, back in the Dark Ages, before the Homecoming dance. We both knew Rune was probably there, and likely other spellspinners as well.

I sighed and rubbed my forehead. Should he have risked his life for a clean shirt? I don't handle tricky moral questions well. I never had to, before I met Lance. Now it seems they're a daily occurrence.

I looked at Raina. "Tell me something," I said. "Were the spellspinners you met way-back-when good people?"

She looked surprised. "Good? They were people, Zara. No better nor worse than others, but different."

"Different how? Other than the powers, I mean."

She glanced from my face to Lance's, then looked at me again. "Apart from the powers, there is no difference. We all are called to the same purpose, and must do good in the world. Deal honorably with friend and foe alike, and charitably with those less fortunate. 'Tis a universal mandate, but the powers change the manner of it."

"The *manner* of it. I don't know what you mean."

"I do," said Lance. He folded the Ray-Bans, slipped them in his jacket pocket, and leaned against the kitchen counter, every little movement as graceful as a deer. "I've been trying to explain it to you. Our rules are not really different from the sticks'. We take and we give. Equal measure."

Raina looked amused. "I believe the idea is to give more than we take, Lance. But yes. A spellspinner has greater powers than most of us have, both to give and to take, and must therefore be mindful of the balance."

"But if you take from one person and give to another, how is that 'balance?'"

"It isn't," said Lance. *You're thinking of the motel guy. You bet I am. And wherever you got those clothes from.*

"Which is why I promised to pay him back," said Lance.

"Who?" said Raina.

"Lance cheated someone out of a hundred bucks, in order to get us here," I said. Anger flashed from Lance's mind to mine. I shrugged. "The time for secrets is past, remember?"

"Dear me." Raina frowned, but she didn't seem that upset. "I'm sure the circumstances were dire."

"They were."

"Well, since you are a minor, Lance, I imagine your uncle will pay the man back on your behalf. But you seem old enough now to face your own responsibilities."

"Of course I am." Lance was really angry now.

"Why should Rune pay?" I argued. "We have to find a way to do it ourselves. We took, so now we have to give. Right?"

"Agreed," said Lance. "But Rune can afford it. A hundred dollars is chump change to him."

"Okay, then we'll owe Rune. But we owe somebody. One or the other."

Lance was miffed, but actually I felt better. It was good to know that my people didn't just trample their way through life, changing things to suit themselves and stealing from everybody.

We left a note for Nonny and headed out on foot to meet Rune. As soon as the three of us stepped out the door, we smelled smoke.

"Grass fire," said Raina.

Lance and I exchanged uneasy glances. Autumn is fire season in California, so an occasional whiff of burning grass is no big deal. But there was more than smoke in the air. There was anger. And sorrow. And menace.

"Wait," I said. I ran back into the house. Nonny's cedar chest crouched in the dimness at the end of the hall outside her bedroom. She kept it locked, but that didn't matter. I touched the lock and it sprang open. I lifted the lid. Reached inside.

My hand went unerringly to the folded square of cloth it sought: my baby blanket. The blanket I'd been wrapped in when Raina left me at the commune gates.

My power stone glowed faintly in the gloom, as if greeting me. I smiled and whispered to it: "Come." The threads pinning the amethyst to the blanket let go. The stone flashed once and disappeared, materializing in the palm of my hand. My fingers closed around it. Strength flowed into me, steadying me for whatever lay ahead. I glanced at the cedar chest. The lid closed at my silent command, the lock went *snick*. All was well. Faint snores still emanated from Nonny's room.

Now I was ready. I slipped my power stone into my jeans pocket and rejoined Lance and Raina. Nobody said a word.

As we headed down the road, we saw blinking lights amid a haze of rising smoke. Fire fighters had arrived and were containing the blaze. It was a grass fire, just as Raina had said, and not a big one. But when we drew closer we saw what had sparked it.

A van had run off the road into the tinder-dry meadow. It sat, drunkenly leaning, in a depression in the field. The fire spread out from there. I felt shock run through

Lance as he realized what had happened. He stopped in his tracks, sucking in a quick breath of air, and instinctively I took his hand—to offer comfort, support, whatever was needed—but of course the instant I touched him our wholesoul connection swamped me with everything Lance was feeling. His thoughts were too chaotic to pick up, but I got his feelings loud and clear, and my own heart raced in response.

Two cars from the sheriff's department were pulling up. Radios crackled. Blue and red lights flashed importantly next to the fire truck's red and white. A couple of guys jumped out and started unrolling yellow tape to block the public—that would be us—from interfering with the scene. I saw the sheriff's expression change as he approached the front of the van. Somebody barked out a cuss word. I closed my eyes, suddenly dizzy from the glimpse I'd had.

The van was not damaged at all. There wasn't a mark on it, apart from the charring where the fire had started. But even with the doors shut, it was clear that the cab was drenched with blood—on the inside. It was thickest on the windshield, which was completely red and a bit lumpy…that's what had made me close my eyes. I did not want to see it. I did not want to think about it. It looked as if the person driving the van had exploded, and the van had drifted on, driverless, until it ran off the road and into the ditch. This would make no sense whatsoever to the sheriff's department, but I knew what had happened, and so did Lance.

"What is it?" whispered Raina. She sounded terrified.

I swallowed and opened my eyes, being careful to look only at Raina, and not at the accident scene. "A spellspinner tried to drive down Chapman Road."

Raina looked bewildered, so I tried to explain. "Lance and I built a shield around Nonny's property. Spellspinners can't cross it. The only way to get past it is to skatch, and Lance and I are the only ones who can do that, because we're the only spellspinners who visited Nonny's property before the shield was built. This is how we've kept the others from bothering Nonny."

She cocked her head like a puppy, trying to follow what I was saying. "So if a spellspinner tried to drive through the shield…"

"The car would pass, no problem," said Lance. "The driver, not so much."

Lance is made of sterner stuff than I am. He was staring at the vehicle, his brows knitted in concentration. "Why a van?" he muttered, seemingly to himself. "Who would be coming here in a van?"

But I had to let go of Lance so I could wrap my arms around my stomach. I was starting to shake. A monstrous thought was forming in the back of my brain. I felt Lance's arm go round my shoulders and he pulled me to him, steadying me. "You're not a murderer, Zara," he said quietly. "They knew about the shield."

"Wh-who knew?" My teeth were chattering.

"Rune. Amber. The other four who went to the Homecoming dance to take you into custody. They snatched you at the dance because they couldn't get at you here, remember?"

"So y-you think it was one of the others? From Spellhaven? S-somebody who didn't know?"

"I suppose. Maybe." He was frowning again. "It doesn't make any sense. Rune should have told everyone. The Council knew for sure. Maybe they didn't understand. They must have thought they could get through it in a vehicle even if they couldn't skatch."

"We should have made sure they understood. It's our fault. We didn't explain it to anybody." I covered my face with my hands, shuddering.

"Zara." Lance's arm, still around my shoulders, gave me a buck-up squeeze. "The shield was a defensive move. If you build a wall to protect yourself, and somebody is so determined to get at you that they smash themselves against the wall, how is that your fault? Get a grip."

Raina's arm, slim and cool, slipped around me from the other side. "He's right, honey."

I gave a shaky laugh. "Okay. Okay. Sorry. I just..." I swallowed hard. "Never mind. Sorry. It's just so awful."

"That it is," Raina agreed. "But be comforted. There are worse deaths. Whoever that was, he — or she — had no time to suffer."

I shivered.

"Look." Raina pointed down the road. Well past the accident scene, a small knot of people stood, motionless, on the gravel at the side of the road. They weren't looking at the accident. They were looking at us.

I recognized a few faces, and was relieved to see Rune's slim, elegant form among them, his silver hair ruffling in the breeze. Amber was there, too, her beautiful face hard with anger, her lithe form clad in something that resembled a catwoman suit. High heeled boots. A mane of auburn hair glinting in the sunlight. Now I wished I had worn something less...meek.

Lance picked up my thoughts and slipped me a sly grin. *My arm's around you, cupcake. Not Amber.*

What an inappropriate time to blush. I pulled away from him — and Raina, too, while I was at it. *Stop distracting me. And don't call me cupcake.*

But I laced my fingers through theirs and felt stronger.

It was eerie, walking hand-in-hand toward the spellspinners, past the horror beside the road. They just stood and waited for us. And we walked toward them. It was like we were on a different planet, totally disconnected from the fire and death and commotion only a few yards away. Only ten or eleven spellspinners were present; not the full contingent by any means. I wondered what that meant, especially for Raina. She would need to tell her story to all forty-eight at some point...oh, wait. Forty-seven now.

The same thought was occurring to Lance. One of us had died in that crash. Maybe more. Did that change the equation? Was there room for me, now, among my kind?

The vibe I was picking up was not exactly welcoming. I didn't see anyone rushing forward with open arms. In fact, nobody cracked a smile.

Lance decided that the best defense was a good offense. He planned to speak first. As soon as we felt the shimmery sensation of the inside of the shield — which we could have walked through, actually, since the shield was built to keep spellspinners out, not in — we stopped. Naturally, Raina couldn't sense the shield, but she stopped when we did. Lance swept his gaze across the grim faces before us and asked, "Which of us was in that van?"

"Nedra," said Rune quietly. "And Peter Carrick."

Vivid images flashed in Lance's mind. Seeing them, fresh fear and horror skittered down my arms. I remembered Nedra, the quiet woman with amethyst eyes — eyes so like mine that I'd wondered if we were cousins. Peter Carrick was not a name I knew, but when I saw Lance's memory of him I recognized him at once. He was the ancient man in the pillow-stuffed carrying chair, whose frail body belied his power. The oldest of the spellspinners. The head of the Council.

Chapter 6

"I'm sorry," I whispered, and meant it. "I'm so sorry."

At that, all the glittering, jewel-colored eyes swiveled from Lance to me, their gazes pinning me. I felt the puzzlement tempering their anger as they pondered what I'd said, weighed my sincerity, recognized — some with reluctance, some with lingering suspicion, some with relief — that I was, in fact, sorry for this loss. That I bore my kinsmen no ill will.

All but Amber, of course. There was no room in her one-track mind to feel anything toward me but enmity, and I had to admit, the feeling was mutual.

Wait a minute. Something was different. The spellspinners were reading me much more clearly than they ever had before. And my sense of them was sharper, too. Even Amber, whose powers were so weak that even to Lance her mind was nearly as opaque as a stick's — even she, I could suddenly read. And she seemed able to pick up a glimmering of my thoughts as well — at least enough to know I was telling the truth.

Knowledge flooded my brain. I knew, without being told, that the oldest, frail Council members were cared for in turns, and that this month had been Nedra's turn to tend to Peter Carrick. She had been driving him. In a van, to accommodate his wheelchair. Why they had been driving toward Nonny's house remained a mystery, since none of the spellspinners present had been told their plans. But it seemed obvious that Peter, as the head of the Council, and Nedra, who shared my relatively-rare amethyst eyes, had taken it upon themselves to…to what? Talk to me, or ambush me? Offer a solution, or take Nonny hostage? Support me, or destroy my home? Their intentions may have been friendly. Their intentions may have been hostile. We would never know.

But they were gone. And with the thinning of our ranks, the remaining spellspinners—including me—had become more powerful.

Interesting.

For the first time, I understood what my existence meant to the rest of the tribe. I'd been draining power from them for sixteen years. No wonder they wanted to eliminate me.

But forty-nine was the magic number. Forty-nine was what everyone agreed on. Forty-nine was the pact. My birth had weakened everyone's powers by illegally boosting the number of spellspinners to fifty…but now…

"Now," I said slowly, "instead of fifty, we number forty-eight."

"Forty-seven," snapped Amber. "You don't count."

I sensed the ripple of annoyance going through the rest of the group. Was Amber oblivious? Evidently. Her yellow cat-eyes narrowed at me and she tossed her hair like a cartoon vixen. "You're not one of us, sugar," she drawled. "You never will be."

Rune's voice was quiet, but we all heard it. "That's enough, Amber."

A woman piped up from the back row. "She's obviously one of us." The murmur of agreement warmed my heart until a man's voice added, "That's not the question."

I looked at all the faces. Even the sympathetic ones were grave. "There's still a question?"

"You shouldn't exist," said Amber. "Period."

Rune looked pained. "Now, Amber—"

She rounded on him, looking ready to spit fire. "Don't you 'now, Amber' me! It's the truth and you know it. We have our laws for a reason. We obey for a reason. What if I randomly reproduced, without the Council's permission? What if you did? Or you?" She whirled around, pointing her beautifully manicured index finger at faces in the group.

"We can't just hook up with anyone who looks interesting! We can't have random babies, who may or may not turn out to be spellsp—" She choked, realizing in the nick of time that she'd nearly shouted out our identity.

Raina's quiet voice halted the tirade. "If Zara should not exist, your quarrel is with her parents. Not with Zara."

All eyes turned to Raina. I sensed them studying her, noting the resemblance to me. Rune, of course, had told them about our phone call, so they were expecting to meet my mother. Puzzlement flickered in their minds. More than one of them thought *sister* so loudly I actually picked up the word.

Raina seemed unfazed by their scrutiny. "I am here," she said. "And I say to you that Zara's birth broke no rules."

Now another word was shining in their minds: *stick.* Some were angry and some were afraid. Nobody was happy. For a stick to speak so casually of spellspinner rules—for a stick to even know spellspinners existed—was a major shock.

"Not here," said Rune. He spoke for everyone. "Such matters should be aired before the Council."

Raina tilted her head like a curious bird. "How do you propose to get me to Spellhaven?" she asked. Her tone was mild and her voice was soft, but most of the spellspinners' faces looked like they'd been slapped. Sticks don't know about Spellhaven. That's the whole point of Spellhaven.

"Or me," I added, claiming their attention while they were still rattled. "My last visit wasn't exactly a vacation in paradise. I'm not eager to repeat it."

Rune's smile was pleasant, but distant. "By tonight, everyone will have assembled in Cherry Glen. Right here in Cherry Glen. We rely on your knowledge of the town, Zara. Find us a safe place to meet. And please refrain from, ah— what's the expression they use in the old movies?"

"Trying something funny," a wry voice suggested from the crowd.

Rune nodded. "Don't try anything funny."

I tried hard not to think, *what's to stop me?*, let alone say it. But I may as well have shouted my defiance. The knot of spellspinners parted, and a thin woman with shoulder-length blonde hair stepped forward. Her right hand was extended like a dancer's, with the tip of her thumb daintily touching the tip of her middle finger, forming an O. And the O made a delicate little bracelet...around Megan O'Shaughnessy's wrist.

My best friend stumbled forward, her mouth working as if she were yelling words, but no sound came out. "Her voice is disabled," the blonde woman said. "Temporarily."

Anger and fear turned me to stone. Temporarily.

All this time, I had worried about Nonny! Nonny had been safely behind the shield. It was Meg, good old Meg, I had left unprotected.

Lance felt my anguish and sent me a warning: *Steady, Zara.* His touch, and the strength I felt flowing into me from him, was the only thing that kept me holding it together. Because my first instinct was to rush forward and break the fingers of the woman who was so casually imprisoning my best, my one true, friend.

Meg was a tiny thing among my tall kinsmen, her red curls tousled and her glasses askew, bare feet planted stubbornly in the meadow grass. She was wearing hideous yellow pajamas dotted with purple cats. They had obviously snatched her right out of bed.

She started crying when she saw me, but she didn't want me to know — as if I wouldn't know anyway! — so she scowled and sniffed hard, then glared at her captors. She didn't seem surprised by my presence. I suppose when a coterie of spellspinners breaks into your bedroom and takes you captive, you figure — if you're Meg — that it has something to do with Zara. And if you've been afraid for a while that you'd never see Zara again, this passes for good news.

Talk about cold comfort.

"Let her go," I said. "She has nothing to do with this."

The blonde gave me a sour smile. "It was you who brought her into it," she said. "By telling her too many secrets."

"She's kept them," I said, anger punching through my voice. "I think you'd better let go of her wrist. There are more cops coming." I pointed down the road behind them.

Is that the oldest trick in the book or what? But it worked. Most of the group, including blondie, glanced over their shoulders to look. They were only distracted for a fraction of a second, but a fraction of a second was all I needed.

My gaze flicked at blondie's fingers. Meg, bless her, was watching me, because she knew I would do something — she just didn't know what. Meg could not feel blondie's spell shattering, but she knew what my glance meant. She yanked her wrist free and ran toward me. The shield, of course, had no effect on her whatsoever.

An old man standing in the front of the group gave a yell and grabbed her, but Raina rushed forward and pulled Meg right out of his grip. Together, they stumbled through the invisible barrier and into a group hug with me — and even Lance, since he didn't want to let go of me.

The old man hit the invisible wall with a grunt and slid to the ground, rubbing his shoulder. A couple of the younger guys helped him back to his feet.

"Wow," I said to the spellspinners, over Meg's shoulder. "You guys really suck at hostage-taking."

Their chagrin was so deep, I almost felt sorry for them.

"We're out of practice," said Rune. "We haven't had to employ such tactics for several centuries."

Blondie was furious, because she knew it was her fault. "We'll get better at it," she snapped. "So don't get cocky."

"You won't need to get better at it," said Lance.

"He's right," I said. "This was a pretty cheap stunt, and completely unnecessary. We *want* to meet with you. It was our idea, remember?"

"We remember," said Rune. His expression was cold. "Were we supposed to follow your lead, like ducklings? Show up at a time and place of your choosing, with no bargaining chips?"

I let them feel my amazement. "We mean you no harm. Don't you get that? I'm trying to save my own life, not endanger yours."

"I will sit among you at the meeting place, if you like," said Raina. A barely-perceptible smile lifted the corners of her mouth. "I volunteer as hostage."

"Don't be ridiculous—" I began, but Rune cut me off by lifting his hand.

"We accept," he said.

A cop car really did come by then, and slowed to look at us. Tension rippled through the spellspinners. The cop on the passenger side rolled down the window. "Everything OK here, folks?"

"Sure," said Lance. We all waved and smiled. The car rolled on, toward the accident scene.

"The rubberneckers will be along soon," said Meg. "And I'm standing here in my jammies. Hello."

She sounded awfully spunky for someone who was imprisoned by a magical spell five minutes ago. Meg is so great.

Lance looked at Rune. "Call us when everyone has arrived. No point in setting anything up until then."

Rune nodded.

"Right. Well. See you later, then," I said brightly. I was still angry.

We turned to go back to the house, but Meg was standing on one leg like a stork, pulling a sticker out of the ball of her foot.

"Come on, pipsqueak," said Lance. "Piggyback." He picked her up like she weighed nothing, and swung her across his back. She locked her legs around his waist and her arms around his neck.

"How undignified," she said. "Thank you." Her face was bright pink. I was glad Lance couldn't read *her* thoughts. I had a pretty good idea of what they were. It isn't every day that Megan O'Shaughnessy gets to lock her legs around a hot boy. I was almost jealous.

Then Lance shot me a sly look and I remembered, duh, that although he couldn't read Meg's thoughts, he could pick up mine. I probably turned about the same color as Meg. "Rats," I muttered. Sometimes I really hate this wholesoul thing.

Meg pointed at the crash site. "What's going on?" she asked. The fire was already out and the fire fighters were packing up. The sheriff's deputies were carefully unloading Peter Carrick's wheelchair from the back of the semi-charred van, and preparing to dust it for fingerprints or something.

"We'll explain back at the house," said Lance. "And, by the way, don't look."

"Look at what?"

"Just don't look," I said.

We were well out of earshot of the spellspinners — who were leaving anyhow — so I felt free to change the subject. "Did you notice how everyone followed Rune's lead? What's up with that?"

"He'll be on the Council now," said Lance.

"No! Really? He's not old enough."

"The Council always needs a lore master. Peter Carrick was a lore master. Rune's the only other one we've got. So he'll go on the Council, and train someone else. Pass the knowledge on to the next generation."

"Have you no written records?" asked Raina.

"None at all," said Lance. "We leave no trace."

Raina's smile was Mona Lisa-like; I couldn't interpret it. And then she said, "Zach will be pleased to hear that."

Which told me, in case I hadn't guessed already, that she was just passing through. She intended to return to the 1700s to be with Zach.

I'd only known my mother for a couple of hours. And I'd certainly gotten along without her just fine until now. Funny, that it could hurt so much — realizing she planned to abandon me again.

Chapter 7

Nonny made tea and lent Meg a pair of slippers. Meg called her mom to tell her where she was. Apparently Meg has been spending a lot of time with Nonny lately—a piece of news I found rather touching—so her whereabouts didn't strike Mrs. O'Shaughnessy as unusual enough to require explanation.

We gathered in the parlor and sank into Nonny's comfortable old furniture. Meg insisted on sitting next to me, so we shared an oversized chair. She said if I started to disappear again, she was going with me this time.

"Thanks, but they can't skatch a stick," I said. I looked at Lance for confirmation. "Can they?"

"No," said Lance and Raina together. Raina smiled slightly, obviously remembering an incident from her own past. "It's been tried."

"I'll bet," said Meg. "Just think how useful it would be, to send people where you wanted them, willy-nilly. You guys should work on it."

"We could make a fortune. Fear of flying? No problem. Bzzt!" I snapped my fingers. "Welcome to Jamaica."

We started giggling. There's nothing like surviving a dangerous morning to make you giddy.

"Come on now, you two," said Nonny, but her eyes were twinkling. "Don't make me come over there."

I felt Lance's puzzlement. I threw a pillow at him. It was supposed to hit him in the face, but he caught it. I rolled my eyes. *Don't spellspinners laugh?*

Not much.

"After this is over," I told him aloud, "we're going to teach you to laugh, Lance. I'm gonna make you human yet."

"Don't count on it, babe."

I threw another pillow.

"Hey!" said Meg. "That was mine."

Lance tossed it back. "Can we talk? The more time goes by, the more antsy the others will get."

"Okay, okay. You talk. We'll listen." I pretended to whisper to Meg, but made sure everyone could hear me say, "He likes that."

"It doesn't sound complicated to me," said Nonny. "All you have to do is get everybody in the same room. Raina explains what happened, and that's that."

"Not quite," said Lance. "First, there's no guarantee they'll believe her. Second, even if she convinces them Zara's birth predates the rules, some will insist the rules still apply."

"Amber," I said.

Lance nodded. "Amber for sure. Maybe more."

"Maybe blondie," I said glumly. "The one who put the whammy on Meg. What's her name?"

Lance lifted an eyebrow at me. "I forget you don't know us all. That was Louise Moon."

"Louise. Battle maiden," murmured Nonny. She has a thing about names.

Meg perked up again. "Does she go by 'Lou'?" she asked, and started singing. "Lou Moon...you saw me standing alone..."

I hit her with the pillow.

Lance ignored the interruption. "Plus, things just got more complicated." He explained about the car crash, and that Nedra and Peter Carrick had died smashing through our barrier. "Two deaths among our number shuffles the deck. So to speak."

I moved restlessly. "I still don't understand why they did it. Didn't they know the shield was there? I thought everyone knew."

"If they'd connected with Rune, he would have reminded them. They must have come straight to find you."

"You think they forgot?"

We stared at each other blankly, trying to figure it out.

"They must have spaced on it," said Meg. "It happens. Or for some reason they thought it wasn't there anymore."

"That sounds more likely," said Lance. "At any rate, this morning there were fifty spellspinners, which is one too many. Now there are forty-eight, which is one too few."

"And we're all more powerful," I added, for the sticks' information. "And will be, until another spellspinner is born. Is that right?"

"Pretty much," said Lance. "I was too young to remember how I felt when you were born. And my powers hadn't manifested yet, so, you know." He shrugged. "I really can't tell you what will happen when a forty-ninth spellspinner is born. Won't happen until next July anyway." He looked from face to face, almost apologetically. Skipping my face, I noticed. "I'm supposed to father the next spellspinner."

Nonny set her teacup down. Meg squeaked. Raina and I said nothing.

"Aren't you a little young?" said Nonny. She wasn't looking at me either.

"It wasn't supposed to happen this soon," said Lance. "But the Council decides these things years in advance. Based on bloodlines."

Raina spoke. "The bloodlines have been shuffled, too." We all looked at her. "If Zara joins your ranks, the calculations must be made anew."

I felt like a huge weight lifted from my shoulders. "That's what I've been saying," I said.

"No it isn't," said Lance.

"Yes it is," I said. "I just didn't say it as well as she did. Who's in line after you and Amber? Maybe they could take your turn. Skip you."

Raina shook her head. "It won't work like that. Everything will change. You bring in completely new blood. If I'm not mistaken, such a thing has not happened for many generations."

"Amber and somebody else, then," I said. I was perfectly willing to let Amber have the next baby, since she seemed so set on it. I just didn't want it to be Lance's baby.

"Was Amber the one in leather?" asked Meg. "Jeez." Her eyes were round with sympathy. "She looked like she wanted to claw you to death."

"She does," I said glumly. "And now you know why."

"At some point, Zara, they will choose you," said Raina.

My mind shied away from that thought. "Whatever," I said, staring at the carpet. "Not for a while, I hope."

"Unless they kill you," said Meg. "It's like, one extreme or the other."

"That's my problem in a nutshell," I agreed.

"Meanwhile," said Raina, "you are tasked with finding a suitable location for tonight's meeting. What are your suggestions?"

Everyone looked at me. "Um," I said. "Do they have to meet around a fire, like they do at Spellhaven? Because there aren't a lot of campfire rings in Cherry Glen."

"There's a fireside room at my church," Meg offered. "It's a nice space."

"Not for this group," said Lance. "But we can go anywhere that's private. No campfire necessary."

"I like the church idea," said Nonny. Her expression was fierce. "It'd be harder for them to condemn my little girl to death with Jesus and all the saints staring down from the walls."

"I wouldn't count on that," said Raina quietly. "The same saints stared down from the walls during the Inquisition, when many a spellspinner was burned alive."

Meg frowned. "Why didn't they skatch?"

"Most could not. 'Twas a rare gift in those days."

"We were more numerous, but less powerful," I told Meg. "Can we move on please? Because if we don't come up with something soon they're going to think I'm 'trying something funny,' like Rune said."

A brief, but intense, discussion ensued. It's surprising how difficult it is to come up with a place in a small town where fifty people can meet secretly on short notice. Even when we chose a meeting time in the wee hours of the morning—since spellspinners don't have to sleep, we're not particular about when we meet—there were very few possibilities. Nonny's meadow probably would have been perfect, but Lance and I objected to lifting the shield. The town square was too public, even in the dead of night. Churches, the library, various rooms at the high school—all would have security cameras to disable, and possibly a janitor or guard. The baseball field at St. Francis—Meg's school—would certainly be deserted at 2:00 a.m., but would also be dark, freezing cold, and uncomfortable. Metal bleachers. No thanks.

Meg suddenly snapped her fingers. "Camp Greenhorn."

"That's two hours up the mountain," I said.

"So? You can all leave at midnight and caravan up there."

"How do we know there's nobody holding a weekend retreat or something?"

Meg rolled her eyes. "You've been there before, Zara. That's where we met, remember?"

"Of course I remember."

"So you can scout it out. Skatch."

Lance frowned. "Wait a minute. I don't want Zara going anywhere by herself today."

"Nor do I," said Nonny.

"Why? What could happen? Meg's right. It'll be brilliant. They even have a campfire ring. It'll be like Spellhaven, but pine forest instead of redwoods. And, you know, regular buildings and stuff."

"Even if it's not booked this weekend, there will be people at the camp," said Nonny. "Caretakers. There must be people who live there year-round."

"Well, we have to meet somewhere, and this is the best idea yet. I'm going to check it out." A chorus of objections rose, but I was sick of objections. I closed my ears and my eyes, quickly pictured the wooden pier jutting into the lake at Camp Greenhorn, and skatched.

Sometime during the four years that had passed since Meg and I met at summer camp, the pier had been removed. I arrived mid-air and dropped into the lake.

The shock punched the air out of my lungs and nearly stopped my heart. The lake was well on its way to freezing, and I had totally not expected to be in it. I kicked frantically toward what I thought was the surface, but maybe I was upside down. I couldn't tell for sure. I couldn't think. I couldn't breathe. I couldn't tell which way was up. Desperate, I skatched home and landed on the rag rug beside my bed, coughing and spitting up water.

They tell me I was only gone for about twenty seconds. It was possibly the longest twenty seconds of my life. And everybody but Meg was mad at me now.

I was not having a good day.

By the time I got out of the hot bath Nonny insisted I take, the meeting place had been chosen without my input. At least my teeth had stopped chattering. Meg was dressed, having helped herself to the few things in my closet that fit her, and her boyfriend Alvin had joined the party. And plans were underway to gather the clan on the Chapmans' property.

The Chapmans are our only neighbors. They have an old barn, no longer used as a barn, in which they sometimes hold dances and parties. They're a lot more social than we are. They actually have friends, like normal people. Nonny knew they were out of town, so she called them up and asked if they'd mind if we held a meeting in their barn. I think she may have left the impression that it was a family reunion or something. Anyhow, they were neighborly enough to say yes and tell us where they kept the keys, so that's where we were headed tonight.

As I entered the parlor Lance's anger pressed against me so hard, it was almost difficult to walk under its weight. I barely had time to say, "Hi, Alvin" before Lance's fingers closed around my upper arm, flooding me with his fury.

"Can I talk to you for a sec?" he said. No one would have guessed from his tone how mad he was. But I had inside information, so to speak. I tried to nod, for the sake of the others who were watching, but I wonder what my expression was. Anyway, he pulled me into the dining room and through the swinging door into the kitchen, where no one could see us.

"I'm *sorry*," I snapped, pulling out of his hold. "I didn't mean to scare everybody. Haven't I been punished enough? I almost drowned."

His kryptonite eyes bored into mine. "Alvin," he said tonelessly. The word focused my scattered brain and I realized what he was really upset about.

"Oh." I crossed my arms, defensively hugging myself. "I forgot you didn't know about him."

"How many others, Zara?" He leaned against the kitchen wall, pinning me with his green, green gaze. I hadn't seen him this angry since that horrible day when he tried to crush my powers. "How many sticks have you told our secrets to?"

Ouch.

"I didn't tell Alvin. I swear." I slid into one of the kitchen chairs, weakened by the pressure of his wrath. "Meg wouldn't either. So Alvin doesn't know anything. At least, he didn't until Homecoming night, and whose fault was that? It was a risk the Council took when they sent you guys to grab me in a public spot. They wanted to expose me, well great, they did. But I'm not the only one they exposed. A bunch of people who never knew we existed now know that we do. It's not my fault. It's theirs."

It was ridiculous to try to hide anything from a boy who could read my mind. I was blocking him as much as I could, but just the fact that he could feel my block told him I was leaving something out.

I dropped my head into my hands so I didn't have to look at his face anymore. "I'm sorry. Okay? It was an accident," I said. I took a deep breath, and just flat-out told him. "Alvin didn't understand what he saw, but he saw something, and he knew it was strange. He caught me skatching. There. Now you know."

When I felt the emotions pouring out of Lance I hurried back into speech. "I still don't think Alvin actually knows anything—other than—well—he obviously knows there's something peculiar about me. And that part is my fault. Obviously. I admit it. But he was at the Homecoming dance, so he knows it's not *just* me. And that's not my fault. Anyhow, there's no point in leaving him out of the loop now."

I sent him the story telepathically, hoping that would give Lance a more complete understanding—at least to reassure him that I hadn't intended to divulge spellspinner secrets. I had just, in a moment of anger (with Lance, of course), skatched a bit hastily. Okay, a lot hastily. And in my eagerness to get away from Lance, I had landed somewhere where I was seen, popping out of thin air. And Alvin was the one who had seen it.

And then I'd compounded the error by skatching to Meg's house one day. She and Alvin were not a thing, at that point. I had no way of knowing she had company. But Alvin had dropped by to see her, and, well, I popped out of thin air again, right in front of him.

"I'm impulsive. You're always telling me that. Well, okay, I see it. You're right. I'm too impulsive. I get emotional, and then I make bad decisions. I'm careless. I'll work on it, I promise."

In the silence that followed, Lance struggled to contain his horror, his fury. I felt every wave of it, beating against me, pushing against my battered psyche. Miserable, I finally lifted my eyes to his. "I know I let you down."

The fact that he had made me miserable tempered his anger with remorse. Just a tad. He lifted one hand in a *stop* gesture and walked away to gaze out the window over the sink, breathing deeply. Finally he let his breath out in a sigh and ran his fingers through the lock of hair that always falls across his forehead, pushing it back. "Zara, Zara, Zara." He shook his head, still staring unseeingly out the window. "What are we gonna do with you?"

Unease prickled along my arms. "What do you mean, 'we?'" I tried to speak lightly. "Don't tell me you're changing sides."

"I can't change sides." He sounded bitter. "You know I can't change sides."

"But you wish you could." I tried not to feel hurt. Failed.

"Of course I wish I could." He turned to face me. Leaning back against the sink, his body was long and lithe and languid, but beneath the surface anger still smoldered. His eyes glittered and I was reminded once again of a jungle cat—lethal power clothed in deceptive grace. "You wish you could, too. But we can't. We're stuck with each other."

Answering anger flickered in me. "That's a fine way to put it."

"It's the truth."

"Are you saying you wish I didn't exist? Because that's what I'm hearing."

He was across the room so fast I wondered if he'd skatched, pulling me up out of the chair. Then his mouth came down on mine and I stopped thinking or wondering about anything. I could hear my heartbeat. I could hear his. Blood roared and pulsed in my ears. His mind fused with mine and we swam together in a mutual sea of desire and confusion, anger and tenderness. I wanted nothing more than to be with Lance. I wanted nothing more than to be free of him. I didn't know what I wanted. I didn't know what he wanted. But the wanting was overwhelming.

He tore his mouth away and pressed his forehead against mine. We hung there, breathing hard, trying to return to earth, trying to regain our wits.

"Zara." His voice croaked. "I think I love you. I just wish I had a choice about it."

I didn't know whether to laugh or cry.

"Me too," I whispered.

Chapter 8

Raina looked fantastic. Meg, Nonny and I had gathered in my room and attended her like bridesmaids as she donned her early 18ᵗʰ century rural Irish I-don't-know-what clothes. The clothes she wore when she arrived from Zach's century. I had to admit, they suited her down to the ground. Plus anyone could tell they were real. If I were the Council, I'd believe her story in a heartbeat.

Meg was thrilled. She circled Raina, rubbing the fabrics between her fingers and asking questions.

"What's this thing?"

"That's my chemise, and you're not supposed to mention it."

Meg laughed. "I wish I had my phone. Zara's is at the police station and Nonny's is so old, it doesn't take decent pictures. That belt is wicked cool."

"Thank you."

I sighed. "Meanwhile, what am I supposed to wear? I don't mean to complain, but you look a lot more impressive than I do."

"Aye, but you can do the impressive things. Not," she added hastily, "that I mean to say you should. Not tonight."

"I'll try not to frighten them," I promised. "Unless they deserve it."

Meg interrupted. "Why do they call the dress a girdle?"

"It's not a girdle, it's a kirtle, and it's actually considered old-fashioned even in 1710. The belt is called a girdle."

"I should be taking notes."

I rolled my eyes. "You'll have to excuse her," I said to Raina. "She's going into Girl Scientist mode. It happens."

The kirtle was cornflower blue, and the belt was a wide, tooled leather affair that cinched her waist and defined her figure. Raina patted it almost affectionately. "I feel more like myself now."

The kirtle was, actually, a thing of beauty. Raina told us that fashions changed in the palaces of Europe, but where she was from, the classics still prevailed. The blue gown was classic, all right—simple and flowing, with a train that Raina caught up and tucked into the belt so it formed a decorative loop against the back and side of her skirt. The kirtle was worn over an ivory-colored chemise—plain, but spotless (thanks to Nonny's washing machine) and elegant with the kirtle over it and just the right amount of skin showing at the neckline. Raina's beautiful hair flowed over her shoulders and down her back—which, she pointed out, was not really acceptable for a married woman in 'her' day, but impressed us twenty-first century types. She wore a silver circlet on her head, with delicate patterns worked into the metal by some ancient craftsman. Soft suede boots completed the ensemble.

"You look like a princess," I said.

"Maid Marian," said Megan dreamily.

"Princess," said Nonny. "That reminds me. Why did you name your baby Zara?"

Raina looked startled. "What do you mean? Why shouldn't I?"

"It means 'princess,'" said Nonny. "Was it a clue?"

A slow smile lit Raina's face. "That's rich. Really?" She laughed softly. "It should have been," she said. "But no. It's the first two letters of Zach's name and the first two letters of my name. Zach-Raina. Za-ra."

"How disappointing," I said, laughing. "I hoped that crown-thing on your head meant I was a princess."

Raina's smile turned mischievous. "No, baby. It means I am. The equivalent, anyhow, where I come from. It's no small thing, to be Zachariah Wilder's woman."

"You realize," I said drily, "that where you come from is actually here. Now."

Raina looked at herself in the mirror. Her eyes went soft with memory. "Then I should have said not, 'where I'm from,' but 'where I belong.'"

Meg shuddered dramatically. "I don't think I could stand it. No plumbing. No deodorant. No internet. No thanks."

"And here? No Zach." Raina made a tiny adjustment to her sleeve, then smiled at Meg. "No contest."

I heard Lance in my head. *Time to go.*

My heart rate sped up. "Are we ready?" I said.

"As ready as we'll ever be," said Nonny.

No one was smiling anymore. "Let's go," I said.

Alvin and Lance were waiting at the foot of the stairs. They hadn't exactly bonded. Alvin looked a bit shell-shocked from his day of total immersion in my world, but his loyalty to Meg kept him stubbornly present, refusing to abandon ship. I like Alvin.

"Here's the deal," I said, before anyone else could start. "Raina has to go before the Council. Lance and I have to go too. None of the rest of you are obligated. In fact, you're not allowed to go, and I don't want to hear a word about it."

Meg's scowl was fierce. She opened her mouth and I put my fingers in my ears. "Literally," I said. "Please. Lance and I don't want to hear about your plans for tonight unless they involve popping corn and watching movies."

Meg closed her mouth. Then she opened it to say, "I get it. They can read your minds."

Lance said, "We have to assume so. We don't know what they can do, because everyone's powers are jacked up a notch."

"Okay." She squared her shoulders. "Popcorn it is. Let's see what's on HBO."

"We don't have HBO," said Nonny.

"Whatever," said Meg.

"Seriously," said Lance. He touched her shoulder. "Stay here. Don't make plans and just hide them from us. Stay here. Be safe."

"Yeah," I said, half hoping she wouldn't listen to us. "Don't try anything funny."

Meg put on her innocent face. "I wouldn't dream of it."

Lance frowned at me. "This is real, Zara. It's not just a matter of everyone's powers being stronger. They'll post lookouts. If any stick approaches the meeting place, they'll be spotted."

What was left of my bravado melted away like snow in summer. Until this moment, I'd been hanging onto the idea—in the back of my mind—that Meg and Alvin would somehow rush in at the last minute and save the day, if the day needed saving. Guess that wasn't such a good idea.

"So I'm on my own?"

My voice sounded smaller and shakier than I'd intended. Meg scowled and shoved her glasses higher on her nose. "Not as long as you've got me," she said.

"No," said Lance flatly. "She can't have you. Too dangerous. For all of us, if that matters. You show up and Zara is toast. End of story."

Meg bit her lip. "Oh."

"Thanks anyway," I said, and hugged her. "Thanks for everything." I'm not usually a hugging kind of person, so Meg was a bit startled, but she hugged me back. Nonny looked pale and tense so I hugged her too. This was a mistake because she started crying. Then Meg started crying.

And for the first time it really hit me that I might not be coming back.

I had known this, of course, at some level. But somehow seeing my loved ones fall apart made it real. Fear reared its ugly head and threatened to paralyze me.

Steady, Zara. Lance's cool, cool fingers brushed my cheek, sending me calm. Lending me strength. I reached up and slipped my fingers through his, taking his hand. And managed to give him a wavering smile.

"Fear nothing," said Raina. "Courage is an armor stronger than steel." She was speaking to Nonny and Meg, but the words helped me too.

The connection between Lance and me hummed with an almost audible vibration. I felt so strong, touching him, that I could no longer imagine defeat. I bent and slipped my power stone into my sock — clever, eh? — and worked it into the hollow of my right ankle. With Lance at my side and the stone pressed against my skin, surely I was invincible. I felt invincible, anyhow — which was why I was able to walk calmly out the door with Lance and Raina instead of, say, bursting into tears, shutting myself in the hall closet, and refusing to come out.

The autumn night was cold and clear, fragrant with a touch of distant wood smoke, the scent of earth and turning leaf and the promise of winter rains ahead. All of nature seemed poised on the brink of change, waiting thirstily for renewal. A few dry leaves still clinging to Nonny's sugar maple rattled and whispered overhead as we walked past, and the fallen leaves scurried ahead of us like ghosts leading the way.

Lance and I held hands, but Raina walked slightly apart. She carried herself like royalty, graceful and calm. There was moonlight, but when we turned to cross the meadow Lance shone a flashlight beam on the narrow path before us. We saw other lights bobbing among the trees that lined the creek at the bottom of the slope. My breath hitched and Lance squeezed my fingers.

Remember how strong we are, Zara. The monsters won't get you.

The monsters are strong too. And we're outnumbered.

He glanced sideways at me. "Last-ditch move? Skatch to your bedroom."

"And where will you be? You can't go to your skatching stone in Spellhaven. They'll immediately surround you."

"I'll be downstairs in your kitchen."

I felt better. It was good to know we had a retreat option. Then my relief faded. "Where does that leave Raina?"

We both knew the answer to that one. Raina would be left behind, to face whatever horror Lance and I had escaped.

I looked at her, gliding along before us in the moonlight like a refugee from a Renaissance painting. She was serene and beautiful...and powerless as a kitten.

"No retreat," I whispered numbly. "We see this through. Whatever happens, we stay to the end."

Lance stopped walking. We stood for a moment, fingers linked, while he reached inside my mind. He turned me toward himself, lifted the flashlight and shone it on my face. Past the glare of the flashlight beam I could see his face, tense and strong and — momentarily — robbed of the aloof cool he usually wore like a second skin. His hand left mine and rose to cup my cheek. His fingers curved, warm against my chilled face. I felt the honesty of his need to know, so I let him in. Just...let him in.

It was the most human part of me, I realized, that had spoken. Lance, spellspinner to the core, was reaching to understand a human instinct that was, to him, irrational and foolhardy. Admirable, yet stupid. To Lance, nothing was more important than self-preservation. He was brave, oh yes—had shown courage in many ways during the time I'd known him. But whatever risks he ran furthered his own goals.

He had put himself on the line for me, but—being Lance—hadn't done any soul-searching about why he'd done it. We'd both assumed that wholesoul meant there was no real difference between saving the other and saving yourself. His instinct to protect me, therefore, didn't count—or so we thought. Now we both saw that maybe it did. That maybe he was more human than he'd wanted to believe.

In a good way, I reminded him. But Lance wasn't so sure.

His lips twisted wryly. *I could be noble but dead. What good is that?*

I smiled and sent his own words back to him. *Fortune favors the brave. That's just another way of saying courage makes you lucky.* "Never be afraid to do the right thing, Lance."

He lifted an eyebrow, still unconvinced. But getting there.

He dropped the flashlight back to the path and took my hand again. "We'll see."

Raina had halted a little further down the path and was watching us curiously. "We're good," I said as we caught up with her. I thought I sounded remarkably cheerful under the circumstances. "Let's go."

The invisible dome Lance and I had placed over Nonny's house curved down and touched the earth right before the creek. Raina felt nothing, of course, but we sensed a shimmer as we walked through. I tried not to think how exposed we were now, on the other side of it, but I couldn't quash the anxiety. I got a little more tense with every step that carried me farther from home and closer to the Chapmans' barn.

I clung to Lance's arm as we trudged uphill from the creek. I could feel the other spellspinners all around us, slipping silently through the trees or striking ahead on the path we followed. We were going to be the last to arrive, I realized—and simultaneously realized the Council had planned it that way. They would meet us in force. No stragglers wandering in late.

Breathe, Lance sent me. I tried to smile at him, but didn't quite succeed.

The huge barn doors were open, spilling warm light onto the hard-packed dirt of the yard in which it stood. It looked deceptively cheery and welcoming. I knew better.

Raina paused. "I thought you had the keys."

Actually, I hadn't even bothered to retrieve them. "Spellspinners don't need keys," I said.

"I see." She floated on toward the barn, queenly and unflappable. I envied her calm.

Two tall men strode toward us. With one smooth motion, each took one of Raina's elbows. Her eyes widened at their touch, and she almost staggered.

"What are you doing?" I demanded. They didn't answer, and their minds were closed to me. To anyone looking on, it would seem they were simply escorting Raina to the barn. But having just endured it myself, I knew captivity when I saw it. They were propelling her, forcing her. "There's no need for that," I said angrily. "She agreed to come."

Rune spoke from the open doorway. "She agreed to come as a hostage," he said. "We take her at her word."

"You don't need a hostage. That's stupid. We're here. We're all here. You got what you wanted."

"Let it be, Zara," said Raina. "They'll not harm me."

But I felt the vibe emanating from the barn, waves of enmity, so strong it was hard to force myself to enter. And I knew she was wrong. They'd harm her in a heartbeat, if they had to. Some of them would harm her even if they didn't have to; the very idea of a stick coming before the Council was anathema to them.

Was this what sickness felt like? I had never been sick, but I was pretty sure that the sensation rolling through me now was nausea. Flashes of light at the edge of my vision made me wonder if I were about to faint. *They'll never let her go,* I told Lance, panic sending my heartbeat racing. *She's not leaving here alive.*

Lance slipped his hand beneath my hair and cupped his fingers around the back of my neck. Warmth and calm poured into me at his touch. *You don't know that,* he sent me. *Be strong, Zara. Stay in the moment. Focus.*

I took a deep, shaky breath and blew it out. *Right. You're right.* We had to get through this somehow, whatever happened. Later—if there was a later—I'd have time for regrets. Time to bash myself on the head for dragging everyone I ever cared about into danger. Right now, I had to keep my wits about me—or I'd have even more to regret.

The barn was an odd combination of cavernous and cozy. The Chapmans had taken out all the horse stalls except for one at the back, which they had outfitted as a kind of bar or something. There was a platform at the side of the room, which seemed to be meant for musicians to set up, and all the rest was a gigantic wooden dance floor scattered with sawdust and bits of broken straw and hay—probably murder on anyone with allergies, but the effect was quaint and it made the barn smell good. An exit at the back was marked "Restrooms." The light came from several enormous wagon wheel chandeliers, bearing lamps that looked like gaslights but weren't. Hay bales were stacked picturesquely here and there against the walls to provide seating.

Amber and a man I didn't know were standing near the door, surveying the room. "Great party space," said the man.

"Yee haw," said Amber sourly.

"It'll do," said Rune. "Come on."

Raina's jailors were propelling her toward the musicians' platform. Lance and I, naturally, followed Raina.

The Council was seating itself on chairs on the platform, and the other spellspinners were moving hay bales away from the sides of the barn and into a semicircle facing the platform. Which was interesting to see, since they moved them without touching them. All of this was happening in relative silence. Lance's touch sent our connection into hyperdrive and I read his thoughts with no effort at all. *You realize what the silence means?* he sent me. *Their powers are strong enough now to communicate the way we do – mind to mind.*

This was disturbing. Just how powerful had our kin become? Some of them had been able to do this a week ago — Council members, for sure — but most had relied on the spoken word, like sticks do.

It was likely that Lance and I were still more powerful than most of the others, and wholesoul could combine our powers in ways unavailable to even the Council. But at some point, the nuclear weaponry argument kicks in: It doesn't matter that you're more powerful than everyone else, once you've reached the point where either of you can destroy the other.

Raina stepped gracefully onto the platform and stood before the Council. Pearl Doyle's sharp blue eyes narrowed as she studied my mother, then glanced at me, as if to compare. "Release her," she said to Raina's captors. "She's not going anywhere."

"Thank you," said Raina calmly. I saw the tension in her shoulders ease and knew her freedom of movement had been restored to her. And why not? The Council could vaporize her long before she reached the door. She untucked the fold of blue cloth at her waist-cinching belt and, with a practiced twitch of the wrist, tossed the kirtle's train to the floor. She looked like something from the pages of a King Arthur story; a queen of ancient times come to stand among us. My heart contracted painfully with a surge of emotion I could not name. Sorrow? Admiration?

I felt Lance exploring my feelings, puzzled but interested. He wanted to support me whatever came, I knew. But the emotions that so often swamped me were mysteries to him. On impulse, I left his side and joined Raina on the platform. She smiled at me and took my hand. "They want to look," I told her. "So we'll let them look."

We faced the room and stood in silence. My kin, seated in a semicircle before us, looked us over with their cold, glittering spellspinner eyes. I saw myself as they saw me: childish, dangerous, rebellious, ignorant. Extra. And Raina beside me, looking exactly like the girl I would be a few years from now — if I were a stick — with a stick's opacity. They could not read her. They did not understand her. Few of them believed her time-travel story. Most of them were really, *really* upset that she was here.

The Council's minds were closed to me. It was strange to see Rune sitting among the white-haired ancients, his face as grave as the others', his thoughts as unreadable. Despite the silver hair, his unlined face and dancer's body was obviously much younger than the other members. He'd probably serve on the Council for the next fifty years. What a weird thought.

Pearl's face was taut with grief. My heart sank as I realized Peter Carrick had been her friend. And what of Nedra? Who mourned for her? My gaze traveled slowly from face to face, but I picked up no information. Just a wall of anger, behind which they hid their deeper feelings, if deeper feelings there were.

Pearl stood. She was wearing the bright turquoise jacket she'd worn in Spellhaven, its cheerful color clashing with her haunted expression. "We will mourn our losses in Spellhaven, not here," she said. "As is proper." Agreement rippled through the spellspinners. "But tonight I lift up their names. Peter Carrick."

Voices and minds echoed in unison. "Peter Carrick." "Nedra Wilder."

Again came the murmur of her name from forty-seven throats. "Nedra Wilder."

Raina and I exchanged startled glances. I remembered Nedra's amethyst eyes, so like my own, and felt gooseflesh rise on my arms. She hadn't lived long enough to discover I shared her name.

In the fraught silence that followed, Raina's gaze traveled from face to face. "Her name was Wilder. Are there other Wilders here?"

Pearl's lips tightened. Another on the Council answered. "She was the last."

"Not quite," said Raina quietly. "Not quite the last." She looked at me.

Her meaning was clear. The jewel-toned eyes, following her lead, all flicked toward me. I felt their gazes like a series of pinpricks, stabbing into me, probing for a likeness, however faint, to Nedra. Finding it. And a ripple of reactions, all slightly different, as I said for the first time: "My name is Zara Wilder."

Chapter 9

I don't know why it surprised me, but as soon as I named myself I felt the tide turning. I literally *felt* it; a wave of amazement, doubt, excitement and relief that the slightest tweak could turn to welcome. Until Amber's voice cut through the rising murmur like a whip.

"Her name is Zara *Norland*." She rose from among them like a spiteful goddess, all auburn hair and golden eyes and fury. Amber was wearing a silk shirt as green as poison, and—as usual—looked magnificent. "I don't care what she calls herself. She's no spellspinner. She's just a stick with powers."

"Sticks have no powers," I said. "Everybody knows that."

I felt Raina's arm slip round my waist. "Some, we have." Amusement lit her voice. What the heck was funny? "None that you need be jealous of."

I glanced quickly at Raina's face. It was Amber she found amusing. Amber's jealousy was so intense, even a stick could see it.

I tried not to feel smug. Amber wanted very badly to deny that she was jealous of me in any way, over any thing. But as the hot words bubbled to her lips, she had enough sense to bite them back. The rest of us could read her now. How inconvenient for Amber.

Raina's voice continued, calm and clear. "A spellspinner's powers are great, but not limitless. It seems that, as a people, you have grown narrow and suspicious. You think the trust that sticks rely on, would weaken you. It's true that sticks have no choice but to trust each other, because we cannot read each other well. But trust can be powerful too. It is a source of power you have long neglected."

They didn't believe a word of it.

For Raina's benefit, I voiced their opinion. "Trust is easily misplaced. There is nothing more dangerous."

"That is true. And yet it bestows, on stick and spellspinner alike, the power to love. And there is nothing more precious."

One of the Council's ancients spoke then, her high, cracked voice carrying like a bell. "We have no reason to trust you, woman. Even to see you here, standing among us, violates the rules that have kept us safe from your kind. It is our way, long held, to keep to ourselves. Our laws of secrecy do not permit you to live. A stick who knows of our existence, knows our names, even speaks of Spellhaven — you are a walking, breathing danger, and everyone here knows it." She pointed a bony finger at me, and her yellow eyes narrowed in her creased face. *Yellow eyes...*I remembered that Amber's great-grandmother was on the Council, and my heart sank. "You, girl. You say you are the daughter of this stick. By what right do you name yourself Wilder?"

Raina spoke before I could gather my wits enough to answer. "Birthright," she said. The gentleness of her tone had hardened, and her words rang loudly, so all could hear. "Do not speak to me of your rules. I was there when they were written. Zara is the trueborn daughter of Zachariah Wilder."

Her words caused a sensation. People gasped, broke into speech. Some leapt from their seats. There was chaos even on the Council. I could make no sense of the cacophony. It was like we instantly deteriorated into a gathering of sticks, losing our cohesion in a muddle of individual reactions. In the midst of it all Raina stood calm, her sustaining arm still lightly circling my waist. We were the only unsurprised people in the room.

Except for Lance. He stepped onto the platform beside me and I felt a tingle of awareness, as if I were a sculpture of steel shavings and he were a magnet. *True north,*

I thought idiotically, and smiled. He heard my thought, of course. *You are my true north.*

His mouth quirked in the crooked smile that made my heart jump. Our fingers seemed to reach, touch, clasp of their own volition. With Lance at my side, and Raina as well, I felt safe. Which was really stupid, because I was far from safe. Still, the illusion persisted. We three stood together and waited for the spellspinners surrounding us to calm down.

It was Rune Donovan who held up his hands for silence. And, eventually, got it. "It falls to me," he said, "to unravel this mystery."

The yellow-eyed crone snapped, "You are not impartial."

"None of us is impartial," said Pearl. "I like the child myself."

I didn't dare smile at her.

"Rune is our lore master now," said another voice from the Council. "Let him speak."

Rune's aquamarine eyes met mine and lit with humor. "You asked me, not long ago, about time travel. Now I see why."

"She did not know," said Raina.

"I suspected," I said. "Odd as that sounds."

Rune held up his hands again. "Let's leave the details for another day. The main point is, Zara's mother claims to be a time traveler."

Disgusted mutters and a few hoots of derision greeted this statement. Rune's eyebrows rose. "My friends," he said drily, "we have long assumed that we are the only sliver of humanity who have powers. Like you, I once thought that time travel was impossible because spellspinners can't do it. There are so many things we can do that others cannot, it seems logical to believe that if anyone could do it, we could. We can't, therefore we suppose no one can. But the *reason* why we can't is that the properties governing this world hold us so lightly. If you or I step into a wormhole, nothing happens." He turned to Raina. "Tell us, if you would, what happens when a stick steps into one."

Her arm left my waist and she moved forward, further into the light where all could see her. "I did not step, exactly. I tripped and fell." Her smile was wry. "And I knew nothing of wormholes, or portals, or whatever you might call them. I thought at first I was having a heart attack. Or that someone had laced my breakfast with LSD."

"What was it like?" Rune's voice was soft, but excitement filled him. We could all feel it. Some even shared his fascination, but I wasn't sure how much I wanted to know. Lance's touch was reassuring. *Can't be worse than watersight,* he sent me. I choked back a nervous laugh.

Raina pressed her palms together, frowning, as she searched for words. "It was like being dropped from a great height. Dropped into the center of a tornado. The world disappeared. There were…flashes of color and glimpses of things, places, whirling all around. Faster than I could see. I felt like I was falling, but without moving. Everything around me was moving." She gave a helpless shrug. "Which makes no sense at all, because of course I was moving. I must have been. I landed on my back in a different time, which was strange enough, but also in a different place, which somehow strikes me as stranger still. I suppose I was lucky I didn't land in the ocean. Perhaps there are no portals over water. I…I don't understand the rules of it, you know. Even now."

"But you came back."

"Twice," she admitted.

"How did you manage that?"

Raina's cheeks pinkened. "Not well," she said. "The first time I tried it, I came back to give birth to Zara. I believed I would take the same journey backwards, you know, retracing my path. I expected to return to the place, and the day, I left. That was why I did not go through the portal until my time was almost upon me. I thought there was little point in going earlier. My plan was not to return to my home, but to get to the highway — less than a mile — and flag down the first vehicle I saw. Drivers who never stop for anyone will stop for a pregnant woman."

"Ah." Rune rubbed his ear. "You counted on the kindness of strangers. And didn't want to go home because you thought, from your family's perspective, in the space of an hour or two you would have grown several years older and heavily pregnant."

"Yes." She spread her hands. "You see my dilemma. Strangers would be easier to face. In my particular situation."

"So you waited until the baby was, ah, imminent — "

"Exactly. Then tried to come back — in the nick of time, as it were — to have the baby in safety, among strangers who would ask no awkward questions, and face the explanations afterward."

"And what happened instead?"

Distress clouded her delicate features. She glanced apologetically at me. "I almost didn't make it. I know now that it was a mad risk to take. I was in labor for hours — I'll never know how long — but only made it to a hospital for the last forty minutes or so. The kind woman who picked me up on the highway drove like a madwoman to get me there. We were both afraid I would deliver the baby in her truck, but in the end, I gave birth in a modern hospital just as I intended." She paused. "A slightly more modern hospital than I'd intended, actually. I overshot my mark by a decade or so. It took everything I had just to find the right place. Finding the right time proved impossible."

Lance's voice was cool, but nowhere near as angry as he felt. "If you'd had Zara in the vortex, she might have died."

"Yes. But I wouldn't have done that," she said. "You don't understand — it wasn't that I couldn't exit. It was trying to find a *particular* exit that was hard. It was obvious almost at once that I would not, as I had thought, return automatically to the spot from whence I came. I walked in and out of many portals, trying to find it. And then, when I was pretty sure I'd found the right place, I kept trying to find the right time…" She shivered, remembering. "It was terrifying. I mean, just a ravine in the woods…there was nothing especially memorable about it. And nothing to mark the century, let alone the year. When I reached the ravine at last, I was so relieved—but then I tried to get to the highway, and the road was nowhere to be found. It simply didn't exist. I have no idea what year it was. I was so frightened…I got lost trying to find my way back to the ravine, and the pains were coming faster…" She crossed her arms over her waist, hugging herself. "It was terrible. When I finally reached the portal, I knew I had to mark it somehow. Zach had given me a dagger as a wedding gift—a silver dagger with a diamond-studded hilt. I drove it into the ground beside the portal."

"Why?" asked Rune. "How did that help?"

"It's impossible to keep your bearings once you step through the time gate. The portals keep appearing and disappearing. I saw the ravine twice more, but without the dagger there. By that, I knew the ravine was either too far in the past or too far in the future. Finally I saw the ravine portal with the dagger just visible—obscured by forest undergrowth and dirt, but there." Her eyes met mine and her lips curved in a strange little smile. "It looked much as it had looked the first time I saw it, winking in a stray shaft of light."

My jaw slackened. "It was *your own dagger* that caught your eye, that day when you went for a walk in the woods? The day you first stepped through the portal?"

She nodded. "Boggles the mind, doesn't it?"

"Woo woo, heebie jeebie," muttered Lance.

"At any rate, I stepped through when I saw the dagger, and headed for the road — and this time, it was there. You can't imagine my relief."

"Very affecting," said Pearl drily. "You should have had the child in the era where you conceived her. You caused a world of trouble, bringing her to the here and now."

"I brought more than Zara," said Raina, lifting her head. Her gaze traveled from face to face, studying the spellspinners as they were studying her. "I brought the power stones of those who would not join. Those who refused, who would not be governed by the Council. They are the stones my husband took by force or forfeit. I brought them far into the future, where the lawless ones could not follow." Her gaze returned to Pearl. "So although I brought a little trouble to this Council, I removed a great danger from the first one."

Something occurred to me, and I blurted it out. "This Council might not even be here, if not for her," I said. "All of you. Maybe you wouldn't have been born. The rebel spellspinners might have escaped their fate, if she hadn't taken their power stones to the future. Then what would have happened?"

A white-haired man on the Council said, "It is not possible to know what would have happened. Speculation is useless."

Lance spoke now. "We know what did happen, and that's enough." His green eyes, hot with suppressed anger, swept the Council members. "Spellspinners have survived three hundred years governed by the Council of Seven that Zachariah Wilder began. I think you owe his wife an apology. Not to mention his daughter." He turned to the room as a whole and let them feel the sense of injustice burning in him. "Is there really any doubt about what's going to happen tonight? We're going to welcome the daughter of Zachariah Wilder into our midst and accept her as one of us. Would you really throw her out? Would you really threaten her life? Wilder's own blood?"

I felt his words strike home. Many of the minds that had been set against me wavered at his words. I was so proud of him.

But Amber wasn't done yet. She leapt in one bound onto the stage and stood by her great-grandmother, her golden eyes glowing with a fury that overtopped Lance's. "She's the daughter of a *stick,*" Amber hissed, making the word sound filthy. "She's not one of us and never will be. I don't care who her father was, and I don't care if they were married or not, this girl is a bastard to the bone. She's a half-breed. She's a mutant. She's a monster."

It was the word 'mutant' that got my Irish up. I was so mad, I acted without thinking—my fatal flaw, as Lance will tell you. I shut that woman up. I mean, I *shut* her *up.* One flick of my eyes, and Amber's too-pretty lips stuck to each other as if they'd been superglued.

Her eyes went wide. "Mmm! Mmm mmm mm mmm mmmmm!" she said. A dozen people in the room shot spells out to free her. I turned them aside with my mind, effortlessly, and their help did not reach her. Lance was sending me, *Stop! Stop!* I ignored him.

"Now, you listen to me," I said, advancing on Amber with as good an imitation of her catlike stalking moves as I could manage. "We've all heard what you have to say. Now you're going to hear what I have to say. Sit down."

She sat. I may have had something to do with how promptly and completely she plopped into Rune's empty chair. Whatever. I was past caring.

"You're not fooling anybody," I told her. "Not even my mother, and she's a stick. You're pea-green with jealousy, pure and simple."

"MMMM—"

"Be still," I said, and silenced her voicebox. Not to hurt her, or damage it. I just immobilized it so the little strings couldn't vibrate. Which is probably what they had done to Meg, earlier, so it served them right to have that little trick played on one of their own. "I'm not saying I'm better than you. I just have something you thought was yours, and you don't know how to get it back while there's still breath in my body. So you want me dead. And you don't much care how it happens, or whether it's fair or unfair. You just want me out of the picture." I leaned over her. "And if you *really* thought I was a stick, we wouldn't have an issue now, would we? No, no, no. It's because you know darn well I'm a spellspinner — and a stronger one than you — that you want me gone."

I straightened, and looked around the room at my kin. "I'm the trueborn daughter of Zachariah Wilder," I said. "My mother was a stick, so I might have been a stick. But I'm not. And if you think there's no stick blood in you — or you — or you — " I pointed at the faces of those who were sending me the worst vibes. "You have another think coming. When I was conceived, there were no rules against spellspinners mating with sticks. Every living spellspinner had a stick grandmother, or great-grandfather, or even a parent. For three hundred years you've guarded your bloodlines, so I'm the last. The last spellspinner born of a stick. But all of you, if you go back far enough, descend from sticks one way or another. So stop saying I'm somehow not 'really' a spellspinner, or that I should die because my parents broke the rules when they had me. My birth broke no rules. There were no rules. And if you doubt that I'm 'really' a spellspinner — doubt no more."

I pulled the power up from the earth, through the barn floor and the platform and the soles of my shoes. It entered me like lightning, shooting through me from my toes to the top of my head. My hair lifted and snapped as if in a wind. Purple witchlight ran along my skin and my eyes glowed like amethyst lamps.

I knew it was impressive, even to spellspinners. It sure impressed Lance when he saw it the first time.

Lance folded his arms across his chest and sighed. *Show-off.*

He was right; I was showing off. He was also right that I should stop, that I was hurting my case, not helping it, by displaying how powerful I am.

But it felt so good.

The power flooded me, filling me with exhilaration. I wanted to shout with joy. I wanted to fly. I wanted to make things happen. Instead, I lifted my arms like a pope blessing the masses and said—my voice echoing strangely as the power infused it—"You are my kinsmen and I mean you no harm." And I sent the power back into the earth.

My hair tumbled down my back. The purple fire left my eyes and evaporated from my skin. I stepped back between Raina and Lance and tried to look humble.

As an afterthought, I released Amber.

The breath whooshed out of her as soon as her lips would open. She rose from the chair, trembling. "And if *that* doesn't convince you how dangerous she is," Amber cried, "Nothing will."

"She showed you her power, and didn't use it," said Lance. "If that doesn't convince you how dangerous she *isn't*, nothing will."

Raina was staring at me, looking a bit dazed. I blushed and hung my head. "Sorry," I muttered. "Didn't mean to scare you."

She patted me wordlessly. I reached out my spellspinner antennae to take the temperature of my kin, and my heart sank. They were blocking me from their thoughts, every one of them. Not a good sign.

Rune studied me gravely. "You are, indeed, a spellspinner. No doubt remains on that point." His gaze traveled slowly round the room. "There are questions still unanswered, however. Not all believe your tale…" His throat worked for a moment while he struggled with what to call Raina. "Mrs. Wilder. If that is, indeed, your name."

Amusement lit Raina's eyes. "I suppose it is, in this century. And now I will tell you why I risked the portal again, to come here and speak with you."

She was not waiting to be questioned, and that bothered him. "Yes," he said grimly. "You will."

She faced the room again and squared her shoulders. "When Zara was conceived, the wars were just ending and the Council had not yet formed. The rules of your society were yet to be written. I tell you truly, I helped Zachariah as he formed the first Council. I helped him lead that effort. And when I left that era so I could have my baby in a hospital, her birth broke no rules. Had I stayed and birthed her in 1704, still no rules would have been broken. But by the time I returned to my husband, it was 1709. The bloodlines had been calculated and the rules were set. No more would stick and spellspinner marry, unless it were a barren match. No more would spellspinners procreate, save by Council decree." She closed her eyes briefly, then opened them again. "I knew not, at that point, whether our child were spellspinner or stick. But I knew she would be in danger if—"

She was interrupted by a commotion near the door. The spellspinners who had marched Raina into the barn were dragging in two struggling figures. My first, confused thought was that they had caught a couple of burglars. Then I recognized them.

It was Meg and Alvin.

Chapter 10

It is completely unlike Meg to do something stupid. Caught between fear for her safety and pure disbelief, all I could do was stand there, horrified, while my best friend and her boyfriend were dragged before the Council and dumped on the platform like sacks of potatoes.

The platform was getting awfully crowded. The audience of spellspinners, however, had vanished. Although there seemed to be quite a few more hay bales, barrels and old chairs than there were a minute ago.

I looked around the room, wondering who was acting stupider, the spellspinners or the sticks. "Is this really necessary?" I said, waving a hand in the general direction of the barrels. "Meg knows a lot of you already."

"It's instinctive," Raina said. "Secrecy."

Unlike the rest, the Council had not hidden themselves with glamours, although I sensed their discomfort at remaining visible to Meg and Alvin. Amber hadn't bothered either. Or maybe she wasn't powerful enough, even now, to cloak herself that way.

My attention returned to Meg. "What were you thinking?" I was furious. "Lance told you not to do this."

"We didn't." She shoved her hands in her pockets and glared at her captors. "These clowns jumped us in the meadow."

I stared at her. Then I stared at them. Their faces gave nothing away, but I picked up a quiver of doubt. Obviously they hadn't caught Meg and Alvin doing anything particularly incriminating.

"What were they doing?" I asked. "I mean, really doing."

"Spying," said one of the guys who had dragged them in.

"We were not," said Alvin hotly.

"We weren't even coming all the way to the creek, I swear," said Meg. "We were just a little anxious, you know—okay, I was. Not so much Alvin. But the idea was to meet you when you headed back to the house, not come to the barn and barge in. We weren't even halfway through the meadow." She waved disdainfully at the two security guys. "These characters came out of nowhere and grabbed us."

Alvin was so pale his freckles stood out like exclamation marks, but he put his arm around Meg to protect her, and stood his ground. "Sorry," he said to me. "I guess we botched it."

Meg looked defensive. "We didn't botch it," she said. "They did."

"But since we're here," said Alvin, straightening his spine and leveling his gaze at the Council, "I'm going to point out that you have our friends. We want them back."

The two guys exchanged incredulous looks. "You mean this is a rescue mission?"

"No," said Meg, at the same time Alvin said, "It is now."

The guys looked at Rune. Rune looked at the Council. Suddenly all the spellspinners were laughing. This I had never imagined. A lot of them looked like they hadn't laughed in years and were out of practice. I even heard muffled snorts coming from a few of the hay bales out in the audience section.

Alvin's face was turning red. "I'm glad you find us amusing," he snapped. "May we go now?"

"No, child." Pearl's voice sounded almost kind. "Nor can you rescue your friends, brave and foolish boy. But now we must decide what to do with you, and I'm afraid you won't care for our decision."

Raina gave a tiny gasp. For the first time, I saw fear in her expression. "No," she said. "This is not the seventeenth century. Your deeds will not go undiscovered. You cannot take human life. I forbid it."

All eyes turned to Raina. The Council was seized with an astonishment and anger so intense that it momentarily froze them. Their eyes sparkled like glowing jewels in their tense, white faces. The very old man who had spoken earlier spoke again. "You forbid it. You?"

"Yes," said Raina. Her voice was low, but she held her head high. "I, on behalf of my husband. We speak with one voice. Though you deny all other authorities on earth or sky or sea, you will heed Zachariah Wilder. There can be no spilling of human blood. That day is past, long past."

Silence. I felt the minds of the spellspinners around me, their thoughts swirling like a storm. First, they had to believe Raina was who she said she was. Some doubted that. Then, they had to believe she spoke the words her husband truly would have spoken, were he here. Finally, they had to accept the authority of the first Head of the Council, Zachariah the Conqueror, Zachariah the Peacemaker, Zachariah the Just. He had been dead for three centuries. Was his word still law?

It was a high hurdle.

Rune sensed which way the wind was blowing, and turned to the Council. "What she says may or may not move you," he said. "But we all know that our powers come with risks. And responsibilities. We might debate for hours and never reach a conclusion, or the Council might take a vote and abide by the majority's will. But I'd like to point out that these kids have kept our existence a secret. Apparently they've been brought here through our error, not theirs. And of all the things that have endangered us, I would argue the most dangerous was our decision to snatch Zara in public."

"Our decision," said another of the Council members drily. "Very diplomatic. You had nothing to do with it."

The oldest man leaned forward in his chair. "What's your advice, Rune? I'd like to hear it."

"We all know what it will be," said Pearl. "But go ahead."

The other spellspinners were dropping their glamours, one by one. Hay bales were becoming seated people. It was an interesting sight. It made you feel as if your eyes had been tricking you — when in fact it was spellspinners who had been tricking your eyes.

"As lore master," said Rune, "I propose that we accept Zara Wilder as one of our own. I will take her under my wing and finish teaching her what she needs to know. She will swear allegiance to the Council, as every spellspinner must. The Council will redraw the bloodlines. As a courtesy to Amber, we shall give her preference, if at all possible, to birth the next spellspinner. But it may or may not be Lance Donovan with whom she is paired."

"And what do we do with the spies?"

"If they promise not to speak of what they saw and heard tonight, let them go. They've done no harm."

Mutters of dissent rose all around us.

"We will debate your proposals," said the old man. "But take the sticks out of the room while we do so."

'The sticks,' it turned out, included me — not a good sign. The guard-guys marched Raina, Meg, Alvin and me outside and left us in the dirt parking lot, then went back in. The barn doors shut, plunging us into near-darkness. Somehow that made it seem even colder.

"It's freezing out here," said Meg.

Alvin put his arm around her. "Shouldn't we make a run for it?" he said.

"Another bad idea," I said. "You're really on a roll. Which reminds me, thanks for the rescue attempt. It made everything worse, but I appreciate the thought."

"I had to try," said Alvin sheepishly.

I looked at Meg. "You told him, right, that these people are creatures of power? You couldn't just stay put, and let Lance handle it if I needed a hero?"

"Hero." Meg made a rude noise.

Raina's mild voice interjected. "He does step up when heroism is called for. You underestimate him, Meg."

I sighed. "She hasn't seen him at his best."

"Anyway," said Meg, "that's what we were doing. We honestly weren't coming to the barn. We were just going to sort of keep an eye on things, from a distance."

"What was the plan?"

Meg pulled Nonny's ancient flip phone out of her pocket and held it up. I groaned.

"It might have helped," said Meg defensively. "Nonny insisted we do something, and this was the only thing we could do. We didn't dare get close enough to really hear anything, or see anything. But if we heard screaming or the place went up in flames, we could call 911. Like, send in the marines."

I covered my face with my hands. "Ai yi yi. Way to get us all killed, Megan."

Raina seemed remarkably calm. "I think they will not harm you now," she said. "Not all believe us yet, but the evidence is strong. I think they must allow for the possibility that what we say is true."

"The possibility," I repeated glumly. "Remember, they're weighing that possibility against a certainty. Sticks know of our existence now. That's a danger to them."

"Ridding the world of the four of us won't solve that problem," said Meg. "They brought it on themselves. The dopes."

She was starting to shiver. I pulled a little energy up from the earth and used it to warm the air around us. It hardly took any effort at all now, with my power stone pressing against my ankle. I could still carry on a conversation.

"Well, Lance and Rune will vote for us, and Amber and her granny will vote against us," I said, mulling it over. "I was getting good vibes from some of the rank and file, but bad vibes from others. I kinda made it worse when I showed off, but you kinda made it better when you told your story. Then Meg and Alvin made it worse again. As for the Council, I don't know. Pearl likes me. That will help."

"Perhaps," said Raina. "She's a cold heart, that one."

"We're a cold-hearted people," I said.

"You're not cold-hearted," said Meg indignantly. She had stopped shivering.

"That's because I'm half human."

"They are all human," said Raina. "Every one of them is part of humankind, however much they would deny it. They like to think of themselves as better than we are, or more evolved, or secretly masters of the world." She sounded disgusted. "They are not."

"Maybe three hundred years ago, they were closer to the rest of humanity," I told her. "But I promise you, the modern variety is a distinct race."

"Of people," she insisted. "A race of people. You're not a different animal."

I let it go. She had a point. Clearly spellspinners were human. But I had inside information, so to speak. There was a difference between my human half and my spellspinner half. Plus I knew the workings of Lance's mind, and beneath all the boy stuff—which was different enough—there was spellspinner stuff. He was cold, amoral and deeply self-centered. How much of that was training and how much was innate, I didn't yet know.

Alvin looked around, seeming puzzled. "Do they have outdoor heaters here or something? It's a lot warmer than it was a minute ago."

"Uh, that would be me," I said. "You're welcome." I wondered where my instinct to hide had gone. A month ago, I never would have used power for such a mundane thing. And if I had, I wouldn't have admitted it to sticks. Last summer, my throat had closed up every time I tried to confide in Meg. I looked at Raina. "I guess you're right," I told her. "The time for secrets is past."

She smiled. "At least among the four of us."

"Yeah," said Meg. "I wouldn't post it on Facebook."

"I never post anything on Facebook."

"I do," said Meg. "But I'll keep your secret identity on the down-low, Batman. In case you were wondering."

"I wasn't wondering," I said. "It's those folks in the barn you have to convince."

Meanwhile, I had my own issues to wrestle with. Like the fact that Lance was sending me nothing. Nothing at all. I reached for his mind and hit a blank wall.

Which meant that the Council was keeping their deliberations a secret, and my boyfriend—bound to me by wholesoul, no less—was bowing to their wishes. Proving once again, in case I didn't already know, that obedience to the Council was more important to him than I was.

This stung. I could simply not imagine ever, under any circumstances, putting the Council higher on my priority list than the people I loved. Or even people I wasn't yet sure I loved, but might probably love someday in the future. Naming no names, of course.

I wished they would just leave me alone. Let me go be a spellspinner on my own terms. Let me and Lance go off somewhere and build a life.

That would be sweet.

After all, Lance could teach me how to be a spellspinner about as well as Rune could. Meanwhile I could teach him how to be human. How to honor the rules that really matter, not the whims of seven random old people. What kind of a system is that? Most of the Council might be senile for all we knew.

And then I felt Lance inside my head. Not words, just a tugging sensation, as if he were invisibly pulling on my arm. "Excuse me," I said, as if I were being called into the next room. "Go ahead and call Nonny. Tell her we're okay. So far."

I sat on a handy boulder and zoned out, concentrating on whatever Lance was sending me.

Well, this was new. He pulled me into his mind and let me see through his eyes. I could hear Meg in the background, talking to Nonny on the phone, but I could also hear Lance speaking.

And see Amber.

They were off by themselves. Where were they? I wondered — then realized they had gone out the restrooms exit at the back of the barn and were facing each other on a narrow path. It was interesting to see Amber through Lance's eyes. She was shorter, and less formidable. Her eyes were glowing like golden lamps, and I had arrived — so to speak — mid-scene.

"Because you're mine, that's why," she was saying. "You've been mine since you were twelve years old."

"Never was," said Lance softly. "Never will be. Give it up, Amber. We're done."

"Done?" She gave a throaty laugh. "Sugar, we haven't even started." Her claw-like nails tapped his cheek and she stroked her hand along his chin. "I've been looking forward to this for years, and so have you."

Lance's hand closed around her wrist. He lifted her hand away from his face. "You're not listening," he said. "I'm not thirteen anymore and easily dazzled."

Her eyes narrowed. "You don't need to be dazzled," she said. "Just obedient. But dazzled is a lot more fun."

Lance's thoughts flashed over to me, warming me all the way to my toes. *Dazzled.* "I agree," said Lance to Amber. He sounded amused. "But I'm dazzled by somebody else." He tossed her hand away and lightly dusted his palms on his jacket. "My priorities have changed, Amber. And they're not changing back."

Amber looked like she wanted to hit him. "It's Zara, isn't it?" she hissed. "Your little crush. The half-breed. The Council may not even let her in."

"They'll let her in. She's a spellspinner."

She tossed her hair back over her shoulder. "If she's a spellspinner, I'm a Zulu. Spellspinners are born. You don't find them under cabbage leaves."

"Zara was born."

"To a stick! They'd be crazy to let her in. And that's not all you have to worry about, Lance. If they do let her in, they may not pair her with you. You may still be stuck with me."

"If they let her in—and they will—she brings a fresh bloodline. They're going to pair her with somebody. Why not me?"

"Because you're *mine*. You've been promised to me."

I felt Lance's exasperation. "Amber. Come on. What do you care? I know it's a big deal to be chosen and all that, but seriously, they'll pair you with somebody. You'll get your chance. Why does it have to be me?"

Amber's fists drummed against his chest. "Because I want you. You!"

Were those tears sparkling in her eyes? Or was she just angry? She sounded angry. I couldn't read her.

Lance gave her shoulders a sharp little shove. Amber stumbled back half a pace. "That's enough," he snapped. "You couldn't care less about me. You just can't stand to lose something you thought was yours. Find yourself a stick boy to play with. We're done."

He turned and walked into the barn, leaving Amber behind him on the path, shouting insults at his back.

That was interesting, I sent him.

Yeah. I'm not seeing her alone again. You're coming with me.

I was so surprised I nearly fell off the rock.

Chapter 11

Maybe I'd made the air a little too warm and comfy in the parking lot. By the time they called for us to come before the Council again, the three sticks had hopped up onto the back of an old flatbed truck and two of the three were asleep. Alvin held Meg cradled against his chest while she dozed, but he was clearly too tense to zone out. Raina lay on her back, her serene face and flowing garments making her look eerily like a sculpture on top of a sarcophagus.

I wondered briefly what time it was. Didn't matter. There was no light in the sky.

"Come on," I said. "It's time."

Raina woke immediately, but Meg was a little tougher to rouse. "'Sup?" she mumbled.

I sent my warming spell back into the earth and let the late-night chill blast her. Her eyes opened. "Good morning, Sunshine," I said. "They're calling us."

Alvin's blue eyes met mine. "I don't hear anything."

"Trust me," I said.

"They sent no guards to escort us," murmured Raina. "A good sign."

I wasn't sure whether the lack of escort was a sign of any kind — good, bad, or otherwise. No point in saying so, of course.

They crawled, slid, stumbled out of the truck. And together we walked to the barn. The door opened as we approached, spilling yellow light across our path. I thought about skatching to my spot on the platform…one final show of defiance. Then discarded the idea — reluctantly — and walked with everyone else, like a good little sheep.

It was impossible to read the faces of the silent gathering, and all their minds, including Lance's, were closed to me. Fear prickled along my skin like gooseflesh. When he sensed my sinking heart, Lance's carefully-shuttered thoughts flicked open for a fraction of a second to send me a beat of reassurance: just the knowledge that this was protocol. When a spellspinner is judged by the Council, no one is allowed to divulge the verdict before the Council speaks.

Oh.

I wondered, fleetingly, who the head of the Council was now that Peter Carrick was gone. My heart sank when Amber's great-granny rose from her chair, assisted by two younger Council members on either side of her. Yep, she'd be the head; she looked to be the oldest. Her malevolent yellow eyes fixed on me, her hostility poorly shielded by her carefully-blank expression.

"Zara Wilder, hear the judgment of the Council," she intoned.

"Hear it," repeated the spellspinners in unison.

"By vote of all assembled here, you are recognized as one of us. It is the judgment of the Council that you be placed under the tutelage of Rune Donovan, lore master and Council member, and that he prepare you to take your place among us. You will come to Spellhaven at the birth of the next spellspinner, join us, and recite your vows. Zara Wilder, do you accept the judgment of this Council?"

An unexpected sense of dread swamped me. Why was I afraid? This was a good thing, right? This was the best possible outcome for me. This is what I had wanted, what Lance had negotiated.

"Yes," I said numbly, trusting that my misgivings were irrational. It wasn't the first time my heart and my head had failed to sync. In fact, I was getting pretty used to the sensation.

The yellow eyes moved on. "Raina Wilder, hear the judgment of the Council."

"Hear it," came the voices again, like a rush of dark wind.

"We accept your daughter, but your testimony is doubted by many. It is therefore our judgment that you lead a party of spellspinners to this wormhole of which you speak, and demonstrate the truth of your words by traveling through time in the presence of witnesses. Raina Wilder, do you accept the judgment of this Council?"

Raina looked troubled. She hesitated. "May I—" she began, but Amber's granny cut her off.

"Answer yes or no."

"Yes, then. My answer is yes."

Meg and Alvin were next. They faced the Council, somehow managing to look scared and defiant at the same time. "Megan O'Shaughnessy and Alvin Carlyle, hear the judgment of the Council."

"Hear it," echoed my newfound kin.

"You have witnessed proceedings that are closed to your kind. You have learned secrets it is forbidden for you to know. The penalty for these transgressions is death. However, the Council recognizes that the fault lies with Zara Wilder, who, in her ignorance, befriended you and exposed our nature and some portion of our powers. You did not seek to know our secrets; they were given to you. Furthermore, you did not come to this assembly of your own will, but were brought here by us, in error. In recognition of your innocence, we extend mercy."

I started to breathe again, but I noticed that Meg and Alvin still looked a tad anxious.

"It is the judgment of this Council that, in lieu of the taking of your lives, you submit to our tampering with your memory—a power we are forbidden to use absent your consent. Megan O'Shaughnessy, do you accept the judgment of this Council?"

Meg and Alvin looked at each other. Then they looked at me. I shrugged helplessly.

"Do I have a choice?" asked Meg.

"You do," said the crone. "Yes or no. That is your choice. Make it now."

"Yes," whispered Meg.

"Alvin Carlyle, do you accept the judgment of this Council?"

Alvin's eyebrows had drawn into a deep frown. He looked fierce and miserable. "If Meg says yes, I say yes."

"I said yes," said Meg.

"Okay. Yes," said Alvin. "What does it mean?"

Nobody answered him. Amber's great-grandmother faced the roomful of spellspinners and lifted her ancient arms. "The Council has delivered its judgment. Let us make it so."

"Be it so," replied the spellspinners. Amber's granny was helped back into her chair. She was trembling slightly from the effort. The woman was really, *really* old — more than a century. It looked to me like her body was wearing out, but her mind was sharp as tacks. Unfortunately, in my opinion. If you have an enemy, it's better to have a slow-witted enemy.

Meg looked around the room, then back at the Council. "Now what?" She sounded nervous. I didn't blame her. "I suppose we're first."

"You are indeed," said an old man with eyes the clear, pale green of chrysoberyl. He chuckled. "No need to be frightened, little girl. We will leave most of your mind intact."

Meg hated to be called 'little girl.' She also hated to be scared. I could almost see her hackles rise. "Big of you," she said, icily polite. "I suppose it does no good to point out that Alvin and I mean you no harm whatsoever."

"No, dearie," said Pearl. "It doesn't." She beckoned them forward. "Just step on up here and relax. Let's get this over with."

I couldn't stand it. "Hold on," I said. "Slow down. What, exactly, did Meg and Alvin just agree to?"

Rune came over and touched my shoulder, a distinctly un-spellspinnerish gesture of comfort. "There is no alternative," he said quietly. "Be still, and recognize that this is the only way we can spare your friends' lives."

I opened my mouth to argue, then closed it again—remembering, with a sudden rush of shame, that their peril was my fault. My eyes were wet. I brushed angrily at the tears. "Well, this sucks," I said.

Meg gave me a quick hug. "I hope I remember you five minutes from now," she said. I think she was trying to make me laugh. It didn't work.

"I hope so too."

Alvin shook my hand. "It's been interesting," he said. I'm not sure he believed anything was really going to happen.

My friends stepped bravely up to face the unknown. I knew what spellspinner power could do, and the knowledge made me wish I shared their ignorance. Lance, who was actually the source of my knowledge—having tried to turn me into a zombie just a few months ago, thank you very much—took Meg's place beside me and slipped his arm around my waist. Even in my highly agitated state, I felt the buzz his touch always gave me. Under the circumstances, it just added to my agitation. My best friend was about to get zapped in some nefarious way, and the boy she had warned me about—the boy she had been *right* to warn me about—was going to comfort me while I watched. How sickening is that?

Wholesoul flickered around us like invisible fire, melting us into one being, but I resisted letting Lance into my thoughts. Not here. Not now. For this ride, I wanted my stick half at the wheel. I wanted solidarity with my BFF, even though—stick-like—she would never know.

The Council moved in silence, surrounding Meg and Alvin. Rune placed his hands on Megan's head, cradling her temples. There came a brilliant flash of light, sparking from seven sets of eyes in unison, in various hues of blue and green, yellow and violet. Meg never made a sound. The light pulsed around her, waxing and waning, the colors shifting.

Alvin looked about as terrified as I felt. Lance was trying to reach me, trying to reassure me, but I kept him out. My emotions were too strong; I couldn't bear to receive comfort from a spellspinner at this moment, even Lance. What they were doing to Meg was evil. It was wrong. They were tampering with her *mind*. It didn't matter that they had—technically—received her permission. Meg had given consent not knowing what she consented to. And what kind of consent is it, when your choice is to consent or die?

The light began to swirl like water going down a drain, and disappeared into the earth. Rune removed his hands and Meg slumped to the floor. Or would have, if Alvin hadn't caught her. His face was so white that his freckles stood out like confetti scattered across his nose and cheekbones.

"What did you do?" he asked, in a high, tight voice. "What in God's Name did you do to her?"

Nobody answered. The two spellspinners who had acted as security for the evening stepped into the circle and took Meg out of Alvin's hands. They carried her to a bench made of hay bales and stretched her out—gently enough. She was unconscious.

I broke from Lance and ran to her. "Meg," I said. "Meg. Meggie." I stroked her forehead, squeezed her hands. She was breathing. Her forehead was cool to the touch. She seemed to be asleep. Lance pulled me away from her.

"Don't wake her," he warned me. "They'd have to do it again."

I stared at him. "Whose side are you on?"

"Yours," he said. "Leave her be. She's fine."

I saw colored light flashing behind me, and turned to see that it was Alvin's turn. Rune's palms pressed against his skull and Alvin hung there, slack, his eyes closed. But unlike Meg, he was moaning a little.

Lance sensed my impulse and grabbed me before I could rush the Council and break up the spell. "They're not hurting him," he said.

"Yes they are!" I twisted in Lance's grasp, but my effort was futile. He was much too strong for me. "I know how it feels. Remember?"

Thanks to wholesoul, my fury and desperation sliced through Lance like physical pain. And what he felt at the memory of what he'd done to me — what he'd *tried* to do to me — was even more painful. This was the first time I'd picked up even a whicker of conscience in Lance, but there it was: the deep red glow of shame. Stronger than remorse, more honest than apology, I felt him cringing inside. He was *ashamed* of what he'd done.

My, my. There was hope for him after all.

But there was no time for us to indulge in the heart-to-heart conversation we obviously needed to have. The colored light faded out and Alvin, unconscious, was carried to the hay bale bench and stretched out beside Meg. Lying motionless side by side, they looked dead. I shuddered.

Rune stepped up beside me, rubbing his own temples. He seemed tired. "Your friend Alvin knew little, and understood less," he said. "But he fought us, which made things difficult."

I clutched his wrist, hoping that the contact would enable me to read his thoughts more clearly. "But what did you *do?*"

"As little as possible." *You're lucky they let me lead.* "If it worked, I blurred their memory of this night. Just that, and no more. They'll know whatever they knew this afternoon."

"Well, good grief. Why do it at all?"

"They'll have no memory of names or faces, or any of the proceedings they witnessed. They won't be able to I.D. any of us in a police lineup."

"You're kidding, right?"

"Yes." But he didn't smile. "Now they'll sleep until morning."

"And then wake up?"

"That's the idea."

"Well," said a gruff voice I'd never heard before. "Let's get 'em into the truck." A woman as big as a lumberjack—and dressed like one, too, in plaid flannel shirt, work jeans and Timberlands—lifted Alvin as if he weighed no more than a doll and headed for the door. Lance carried Meg with similar ease.

I was momentarily impressed, until I realized that spellspinners have the power to render any burden nearly weightless. Duh.

I suddenly noticed that the barn was all but empty. Raina stood nearby, her expression grave, retucking her train through the loop at her waist. Two or three spellspinners were heading silently for the parking lot. Pearl had taken Rune's arm and they were following the lumberjack woman. Everyone else, including the other five members of the Council, had vanished.

Raina caught my puzzled expression and almost smiled. "They had other places to be, I suppose. Now that their business here is finished."

So, yeah. They had all skatched home. Or wherever.

"Everyone but me knows what's going on," I complained, turning out the lights and trailing after Lance.

"You'll catch up, cupcake." Lance jerked his chin at the flatbed truck where the sticks had been dozing a half hour ago. "Make yourself useful. Climb in and help."

"Cupcake," I muttered, disgusted. But I climbed into the back of the truck. Rune handed Raina up, as smoothly as if he'd attended ladies in kirtles all his life. We sat with our backs against the cab, and my limp, slumbering friends were passed in. Raina and I cradled their heads in our laps.

"Good job," said the giantess. She was the only musclebound spellspinner I'd ever seen. She stuck a hand over the slats beside us to shake our hands. "Beryl Alston," she said.

"Zara Wilder," I said. "But you know that."

"Call me Raina," said my mother.

Beryl gave a curt nod and climbed into the cab. On the passenger side, Rune helped Pearl in, then hopped in and slammed the door. Lance joined the rest of us in the back end. The engine coughed, then roared into life and we rocked and bumped slowly down the long, dirt driveway toward Chapman Road. Just as we were turning the corner, I remembered to send a flick of Power back to the barn and lock the doors.

I thought surely all the noise and motion would wake Meg and Alvin, but it didn't. Theirs was not a natural sleep. Still, I didn't want to shout over the engine.

Where are we going? I asked Lance silently.

Your house, he told me.

I frowned. Once Rune, Pearl and Beryl had been to my house, they would be able to return any time they wanted, by skatching. I wasn't crazy about that idea.

Can't be helped, he told me. *Blame your friends.*

Great. I frowned all the way down the driveway, which was probably a quarter of a mile. When we reached the pavement Beryl turned left, but didn't exactly step on the gas. We lurched and crawled down the dark road for another few minutes. When Norland's Nursery came into view, Beryl pulled over and killed the engine. Her door creaked open, then slammed. Her wide, homely face appeared beside me. "Where's that shield you built?"

"Oh. Uh, probably right about there." I pointed sheepishly at the place where Nonny's graveled driveway met the road. "Is that why we stopped?"

"Yep. You're gonna have to take it down, kids."

My frown returned. "Now, wait a minute—"

"No, she's right," said Lance. "We can only cross it by skatching. How are we going to get Meg and Alvin to the house? Besides, we don't need it anymore. Come on." He vaulted lightly over the side of the truck and lifted his arms to catch me.

I was still scowling, but I couldn't think of any rational objection. Believe me, that didn't improve my attitude. I was feeling grumpier every minute. I carefully set Meg's head down, stood, dusted my hands, and jumped into Lance's arms, figuring the force of my impact would probably knock him down. It didn't. He caught me.

"Show-off," I muttered.

Behind us, Beryl killed the headlights, plunging us into darkness. I heard Rune's door open. "Lance," he said. "Hang on."

Rune fumbled with his clothing for a moment and pulled something out from beneath his shirt. Then he tossed the something to Lance. It looked like he was throwing a piece of gravel, but I caught a green sparkle winking at me mid-air and knew it was Lance's power stone. Lance's fist closed around it. "Thanks," he said.

I cut my eyes at him. "Well, well. Easy come, easy go."

He grinned. "You were expecting a ceremony of some kind?"

"Something," I admitted. "It was kind of a big deal. Wasn't it?"

"To me." *To us.* "Not to them." He slipped it in his pocket.

We walked into the waist-high weeds until we were out of earshot. Then we kicked off our shoes, and stood side by side on the cold, damp earth. I sighed and shook my head. "I hope you're right about this," I said.

"I am, babe."

I looked daggers at him—but Lance just smiled and took my hand, and suddenly I couldn't remember what I was upset about. I'd been shutting him out for the past half hour or so, but that was no longer possible once we touched, skin to skin. So for the first time, I got a true reading on just how relieved Lance was—how *glad* he was—that the other spellspinners had accepted me.

And he got a true reading on my mixed emotions about the whole thing. So basically, we were both a little surprised. He stared at me, his smile fading.

"Later," I said, embarrassed that I'd been caught with my negative emotions showing. "We'll sort it out. Let's do this thing before our toes freeze."

Not that I knew how to take down a magical shield, of course. So I followed Lance's lead. We lifted our arms to shoulder height, palms facing the Norland property, and reached out our senses to find the barrier.

"Feel it?" murmured Lance.

I did. It surrounded Nonny's land like a shivering, invisible force field—a bit more ragged, I thought, than it had been when we built it. If the other spellspinners had been able to sense it, there were probably holes they could have walked through. Good thing they hadn't. But if Lance were right, it didn't matter now.

I sure hoped Lance was right.

"I feel it," I said.

Here we go. Lance's shoulder touched mine and our minds connected, fused in a single purpose. Power rose from the earth, slammed into our bare feet and shot right through us. Purple and green light sparked down our arms and arced from our fingertips. My hair lifted and lashed around my face, crackling with amethyst sparks. I laughed for sheer joy; it was amazing. I felt invincible.

When we built the shield, we had had only one power stone between us. With both stones, our power doubled. It was fantastic. And quick. The shield flashed, visible for a fraction of a second, like a ring of purple and green lightning. And then it was gone, streaking back into the earth from whence it came.

We sent the Power back through the soles of our feet into the planet. My hair dropped down my back and the gem-colored light stopped fizzing along my skin. I took a deep breath and let it out in a sigh.

Lance and I grinned at each other.

"That. Was. Great," I said. "We should do this sort of thing more often."

He lifted one finger and tipped my chin up. "We should do this more often," he said, and kissed me.

Okay, I admit it. He caught me at a vulnerable moment. I'd had a stressful night, just topped off by an enormous power rush, largely fueled by wholesoul. Does that excuse my reaction — or even explain it?

Maybe, maybe not. Who cares.

I melted into Lance's arms like butter on hot toast.

The instant I let my guard down, Lance invaded my being. Heat flooded me as his desire — so much greater than my own — blew its hot breath against the flickering, wavering pilot light of my attraction to him. I could almost hear the *whoosh* as the wall I'd built around my heart to keep him out burst into flames. All my misgivings vanished in a rush of fire. Mindless, reckless craving roared within me like a furnace. I gasped and clung to him. I couldn't press enough of him against me. I poured my body along his, chest and hip and thigh, molding myself to him — and felt him pulling me tighter, tighter.

It was too much. I wasn't ready for it. I wasn't *there* yet. I was sixteen and untouched — by him, by this, by most of life itself. And yet I was dizzy with wanting him. And this was more than blind desire, it was *us*.

I wanted Lance. Lance wanted Zara. We shared a bone-deep knowledge that what we felt, we felt for each other.

It would never be this way with anyone else. Not for him, and not for me. Not now. Not ever.

Lance pulled his mouth from mine and rested his forehead against the top of my head. Our breath was as ragged as if we'd just run up three flights of stairs. "Zara," he said hoarsely. Then again: "Zara." I felt his lips in my hair as he kissed my temple.

I pressed my nose to the hollow of his throat. He smelled divine. I tried in vain to gather my wits. Nothing seemed to matter apart from this moment. I was right where I wanted to be. I wanted nothing more than for time to stop. Or better yet, go on without me. Just leave me here, in Lance's arms, standing waist-deep in weeds, barefooted in a meadow in the darkness before dawn.

He sensed my thoughts and smiled against my ear. His hands came up and he threaded his fingers through my hair, leaning back to look into my face. There was just enough light to read his expression. Tenderness looked good on him. The strong, clean planes of his face. His green, green eyes. The lock of chestnut hair that always dropped across his forehead. I reached up and shoved it back into place. "Slob," I murmured.

Meanwhile, back on planet Earth, Beryl tooted the horn.

"Way to wake the neighborhood," I said. As if in answer, the Chapmans' rooster crowed like a freaking trumpet. We were laughing as we grabbed our shoes and walked back to the truck.

Chapter 12

The eastern sky was more gray than black by the time we had settled Meg on Nonny's couch with a pillow beneath her slumbering head and a quilt tossed over her. Raina looked dead on her feet, so I sent her upstairs to my bed. Nonny was a wreck, especially when she saw me heading for the door with Lance, but I gave her my solemn promise that we'd be right back after we dropped off Alvin. So she staggered off to bed too.

Sticks are so fragile.

Beryl, Pearl and Rune took the truck and drove off in search of breakfast. Lance rifled through Alvin's jacket and confiscated his keys. We placed him as carefully as we could in the back end of his open-top jeep-thing, and hopped in front. "This should be fun," remarked Lance, firing up the engine. I grabbed the roll bar and hung on for dear life as we roared and rattled all the way to Parsons Drive. Alvin didn't stir at all.

Lance pulled the jeep up and parked it three doors down from the Carlyles' house.

"Okay. Why?" I said.

"In case his dad is awake, listening. I've heard that parents do that."

The engine did make a unique sound.

"Good thinking."

And just in case nosy neighbors were up at the crack of dawn, peeking through their blinds, we carried Alvin together—instead of using Power to make him featherweight. I took his legs and Lance took him under the arms. In complete silence we lugged him to his own porch and laid him gently down with his head pillowed on the welcome mat.

So basically, Alvin would wake up on his own porch unharmed — but with no idea how he got there.

It was like the best prank *ever*.

By this time, the sky had turned pink and gold and I was biting my lip to keep from laughing. Lance held Alvin's keys high in the air, grinned at me, then dropped them in plain sight, on the middle step leading up to the porch. And then we ran to the side of the house, dropped down on all fours (to be out of sight of the windows), and skatched back to Nonny's porch steps. Where I promptly collapsed in a fit of the giggles. Even Lance was laughing, in his quiet, spellspinnerish way.

I punched his arm. "Is that the hardest you can laugh? You're killing me." I wiped my eyes on my sleeve and tried to catch my breath.

Behind us, the screen door squeaked. Pearl came out, warming her hands on a paper coffee cup. My laughter dried up immediately. "I thought you went for breakfast."

"We found a Denny's down the road a ways. The others are still there, but all I needed was this." She lifted the cup in a toast. "Not much of a town, is it?"

"We like it that way." I hated knowing that she had skatched from Denny's to my house. My home! I felt...invaded. That's what comes of inviting spellspinners in. Once they're in, they can always return.

Pearl gave me a shrewd, sideways look. "You don't care much for me bein' here," she remarked. "Don't need to reach into your mind to read that, child. It's all over your face." She blew on her coffee, then took a sip. "Can't say I blame you."

She sat in one of Nonny's wicker rockers. Most spellspinners are tall, but Pearl's white Keds barely touched the floor. She set her cup on the glass-topped coffee table and rocked back, sighing. "Sometimes I think I've lived too long."

To my surprise, Lance gave a snort of laughter. "What a crock." He stood in one fluid movement, then pulled me to my feet. "Don't fall for her little old lady routine," he advised me. "Pearl's a tough bird."

There was definitely something birdlike about Pearl Doyle. She cocked her head and looked up at Lance, her aquamarine eyes twinkling. "Sit down, smarty. You too." She nodded at me. "You're not out of the woods yet."

We sat across from her. "How bizarre," I remarked. "Out of the woods. That's exactly where I thought I was."

"Ha," said Pearl. "You're not."

"What's left?" said Lance. "Zara's a spellspinner. Case closed."

She studied us, her gaze flicking from Lance's face to mine, then back to Lance. "Hmf," she said. She looked at me again. "He doesn't tell you everything, does he? You're in, but the vote was a squeaker. Not everyone is jumping for joy." Her bright blue eyes pinned me like a bug on posterboard. "And the last time I checked, you weren't so keen on the idea yourself."

I shifted uncomfortably in my chair. "I was your prisoner, remember? You didn't strike me as very nice people."

"Rubbish. You told Lance all summer long that you didn't want to be a spellspinner. You knew nothing about us. You just hated the very notion of us. Well? How do you feel about it now? We haven't given you much reason to change your mind."

You sure haven't. "What's your point?" I asked frostily. "You voted me in. I'm in. Some of you don't want me. Fine. I'm not thrilled about it either. But Lance is right. The Council is right. Like it or hate it, I'm a spellspinner. I guess we all have to get used to it. But you know what?" I leaned forward, eyes narrowing. "I'm a stick just as much as I'm a spellspinner, and you'll have to get used to that too. I'm not giving up my life. Period."

"Well, now, don't get your knickers in a twist. We all have lives." She waved her hand dismissively. "No reason why you can't live as you please. Most ways. Just a few new rules. Nothing to—"

The screen door squeaked. Pearl stopped speaking as abruptly as if someone had flipped a switch. Meg staggered out, yawning. She had a quilt wrapped around her like a shawl. A shawl with a train.

"You're up early," I said.

She blinked at me groggily. "Not as early as you." Her eyes lit on Pearl and she pulled the quilt a little tighter. "Oh. Hello. Sorry." She started to back into the house but hit the screen door with her hip.

"Did we wake you?" asked Lance, while Meg fumbled with the door.

"Nah. I don't think so." She got the door open. "Weird dreams." Her eyes lit on Pearl again. Confusion flitted briefly across her sleepy face. She opened her mouth to say something, then seemed to think better of it. "Really weird dreams. I think I'll go back to bed." The door was closing when she stopped and stuck her head back through. "Why am I on the couch?" she asked me.

"Raina's in my bed," I said.

"Who?"

"Raina. You met her yesterday."

"Oh. Okay." She closed the door.

The three of us looked at each other. "I don't think she recognized you," I whispered to Pearl. "She even seemed a little fuzzy on the Raina concept."

"Looks that way. We'll see."

I was glad Meg recognized me at least. One less worry.

By the time the sticks dragged themselves out of bed, it was nearly noon. Alvin's dad had called around nine o'clock and left a message for Nonny, so her first task was to soothe an angry parent. Alvin had been found unconscious on the welcome mat, and his dad had actually had the phone in his hand to call 911 when Alvin opened his eyes, looked at him, and said, "Where am I?" Just like in the movies.

Nonny had to swear up and down that Alvin hadn't been drinking or drugging. But then she had to admit that she hadn't watched his every move. Which made Alvin's dad think she was a gullible fool who wasn't capable of supervising teenagers. I don't think those were his exact words, but that was her report when she got off the phone. She was all ruffled up like a poked hen. I put my arm around her shoulders and gave her a hug. "Well, talking Mr. Carlyle down was a tough job, but somebody had to do it. You took one for the team."

"Team." Nonny snorted. "I did it for you, missy, but don't put me through that again."

"I won't."

We were all out on the porch by then. Beryl and Rune had departed in Beryl's old flatbed truck, but returned in a gleaming, brand-new seven-passenger SUV. No explanation was offered, and nobody asked. But the spellspinners knew they'd get an earful from me once we hit the road.

The adults were bent over an old paper map of the Pacific Northwest someone had laid out on the glass coffee table, trying to figure out where Raina's portal was and which route would be best to take.

Meg was curled on the swing, clutching a mug of strong black coffee. She still looked like she'd been walloped over the head with a two by four. While the adults were all distracted with the map discussion, I went to sit beside her. I nudged her with my elbow. "You okay?"

"Sure." She took another sip of coffee, frowning. "I just can't seem to remember much about last night. I guess I fell asleep right after you guys left, but that's a pretty strange thing to do. You sure I wasn't drugged?"

"You weren't drugged, Meggie. But stop reaching for that memory, okay?"

She shoved her glasses higher on her nose and stared at me. "Why?"

"Because if it all comes back to you, they'll put the whammy on you again. And it might be worse than the first time. So just let it go. Please. And make sure Alvin does too."

Her eyes widened. "Really? Wow." She sat back in her chair. "Somebody put the whammy on me. Awesome."

I choked back a laugh. "If I knew you liked having your memory wiped, we could have added it to our list of experiments summer before last."

"Adding stuff *to* my memory would be more useful. Mr. Gaskins' English history exam about killed me."

"I'll make sure I learn how to do that. You'll sail through med school." I noted the faraway look in her eyes and poked her again. "You're trying to remember last night, aren't you? Stop it."

"We must have done something amazing."

"It wasn't amazing," I said firmly. "It was stupid. Let it go."

Pearl was watching us from across the porch. "You all packed, Zara?" she called.

"Packed? What for? I'll be home every night."

A brief silence fell. Rune and Beryl looked at each other. I tried to reach for Lance's thoughts, but all I picked up was how hot I looked. Gratifying, but not helpful.

Pearl's ice-blue eyes bored into mine. "Walk with me, child," she said, holding out her hand.

Unless I wanted to look like a brat, which the spellspinners already thought I was, I had little choice but to go to her and haul her out of her chair. As soon as our hands touched, I sensed her thoughts. I didn't pick up words, like I could with Lance, but I definitely felt her warning me to say nothing until we were out of earshot.

She took my arm, as if she were too frail to navigate the porch steps by herself — which she isn't — and basically frog-marched me down the gravel driveway. Her head barely came up to my chin and the fingers tucked around my elbow were so thin they were almost clawlike, but I wasn't fooled. Pearl is strong enough to run circles around people half her age.

"Okay," I said. "What?"

"Can't talk to you in front of all those sticks," Pearl said, vaguely waving her hand back toward the porch. "Nor that boyfriend of yours." She peered up at me. "Is he with you now, listening to us?"

I looked away, uncomfortable. "No," I said shortly.

"But he could be, couldn't he?" She chuckled. "I thought so. Well, well. This is a pretty kettle of fish."

"I don't even know what that means."

"It means trouble," she said tartly. "Probably feels like starlight and rainbows, but believe you me, once the word gets out that the two of you have wholesoul, a lot of folks who just voted to accept you are going to regret that vote. And you barely had enough votes to begin with."

I stopped in my tracks, the better to face her. "Look," I said. "You can't have a do-over. This is America. I can't be tried twice for the same crime."

She chuckled again. "That's so. But there are some who will be itching to find a new crime to charge you with."

"Amber," I said.

"Amber for sure," she agreed. "She'll do you a mischief if she can."

"But can she?" I couldn't help sounding exasperated. "Lance told me she'd follow orders. He told me all I had to do was convince the Council. I thought that was the whole point of having a Council. You guys lay down the law and everybody falls in line."

"More or less," said Pearl. She sounded perfectly cheerful. "If Amber defies the Council, she'll face consequences, and she knows it. Might be she'll calm down and keep her distance."

"And if she doesn't?"

"We'll cross that bridge when we come to it. It's a pity you provoked her. She's always had a temper."

I stared at her. "How, exactly, did I provoke Amber?"

"First you were born. Then you grew up."

I didn't know whether to laugh or punch something. "I'm getting pretty tired of being blamed for stuff I can't help. I can't help being a spellspinner."

"She might not have had a problem with that, if it weren't for Lance. The girl wants Lance. Now she can't have him."

"You got that right." I sounded fiercer than I meant to sound, but sometimes ferocity is called for. I kicked a stone in the path and sent it bouncing down the driveway. "Not that I had any choice about that either. Neither one of us wanted this, or did something to make it happen. It just *was*. We're not doing it on purpose."

"Oh, no doubt. No doubt." She rocked back on her heels, thinking. "If the tales are true, you don't choose wholesoul — and you can't get rid of it, either. Only one thing can break the link."

I raised an eyebrow. "And that would be...?"

"Death." Pearl's smile was serene. "Which is why I said you're not out of the woods. Not by a long chalk. Once everyone knows you two have wholesoul, mark my words, there'll be hell to pay."

I stared at her in amazement. "Seriously? That's insane. Lance and I have no plans to conquer the world. We're not threatening anybody."

"My dear girl, you misunderstand. You don't have to threaten us, for us to feel threatened. It's as if the rest of us have rifles and you two have a nuke. Naturally we would all sleep a little easier at night if that nuke didn't exist."

I threw my hands up in the air. "What part of 'we can't help it' do you not get? You want us to promise not to hurt you? We'll promise. You want us to sign something? We'll sign it. Jeez."

Her eyes narrowed. "Don't be flip. It's unbecoming. You're far too powerful to behave like a thwarted child."

"Powerful." I clutched my head so it wouldn't explode. "For the record, I am refraining at this very minute from demonstrating my *vast power* by, I don't know, rolling on the ground kicking and screaming."

Now she looked amused. "I forget how young you are," she remarked. "We haven't many young people, as you've no doubt noticed."

"Well, this young person has about reached her limit."

"In that case, you won't like what I'm about to say." She jammed her hands into her jacket pockets. "You won't be skatching home during this trip, Zara. Tap into that stick half of you, because you're going to need it. We'll be hitting the road for a few days like a family on vacation. None of us is familiar with the terrain, and we'll have Raina with us, who can't skatch in any case. So we're going to stick together. In other words, child, pack. You'll need your things."

I was furious. "Has Lance agreed to this?"

Pearl sighed. "Have you learned nothing? What is rule number one, for spellspinners?"

I said it through clenched teeth. "Aim for the minimum."

She nodded. "There's no sense in exposing ourselves. Skatching is risky. You've only known how to do it since July, and you've already been caught a time or two. We'll make this journey the old-fashioned way. And we'll keep an eye on each other." Her smile was grim.

She meant, of course, that they'd keep an eye on me. In fact, there was no earthly reason for Pearl to go on this trip at all — or Beryl, for that matter. The spellspinners were triple-teaming me. And, to a lesser extent, Lance.

"I get it," I said. "But I don't like it."

"You don't have to like it," said Pearl. "Go pack."

I stalked back to the house, fuming. Lance took one look at my face and rose out of his chair. *What's going on?*

I glared at him. "Come upstairs and help me pack."

"I'll help too." Meg abandoned her coffee and trailed after us. She shut my bedroom door before I could slam it. I pulled my one-and-only suitcase out of the back of my closet and threw it on the bed.

Lance leaned against the doorjamb, looking amused. "I can't help you if you won't let me in, babe. You should have taken me with you. What did Pearl say?"

"Yeah," echoed Meg, plopping down next to the suitcase. "What did Pearl say?"

I struggled futilely with the locks, then remembered who I was. At a glance, the locks sprang smoothly open and my suitcase yawned wide. I pointed at it. "Now, *that's* power," I said sarcastically, and marched back to my closet.

"It is, actually," said Meg. "I can't do it. Now tell us what Pearl said."

"Nothing much." I grabbed a pair of jeans and tossed them over my shoulder. "Just that everybody hates me for no reason. And I'm basically a prisoner again." I turned around and chucked a stack of folded tees and turtlenecks into the suitcase. They landed perfectly. Or almost perfectly.

I stuck my head out of the closet so I could look Lance in the eyes. "You too, I think."

One eyebrow climbed. "Why me?"

"Because you're my boyfriend." *And they know we have wholesoul.*

Lance swore softly.

"Yeah," I said. "Guess we weren't as subtle about that as we thought we were."

"Wait." Meg shoved her glasses higher on her nose. Her eyes went from me to Lance and back again. "Did I know this yesterday? I mean, I kind of thought things were heading that way, but—"

"I barely knew it myself yesterday," I assured her. "In fact—" I glared at Lance again. "It may not be a done deal, even now."

As usual, Lance looked completely unfazed. "Oh, it's a done deal, babe," he said. "You can't fight destiny."

Meg laughed, but I didn't. "Even sticks can fight destiny," I said. "And sometimes win."

His wicked eyes gleamed. "If they win, it wasn't destiny."

Just looking into his kryptonite eyes gave me such a rush I couldn't follow my own argument. I ducked back into the closet before I completely lost my wits. "You're weak, Zara," I muttered as I dug through my clothes. "Weak."

"But what's going *on?*" Meg's voice was plaintive.

"Well, that's the thing. We don't know." I emerged from the closet with my arms full of wandering-in-the-woods gear. The closest I had to it, anyhow. "We're off to find Raina's wormhole. You remember Raina's my mother, right?"

"Yeah. Freaky."

"Well, she has to prove it by disappearing into the mists of time or something." I dropped the clothes on my bed and waved my arm dramatically. "Thus will she prove that she's a time traveler. How that proves anything else, I'll never know, but the time travel seems to be the only part of her story the spellspinners have a problem with. If a stick can vanish through a wormhole, suddenly it all makes perfect sense to them. Go figure."

"You have to admit, it's hard to believe she's your mother." Meg was refolding my shirts and tucking them neatly in the suitcase. "Why don't they insist on a DNA test?"

I rolled my eyes. "Too scientific. Too logical."

"Too slow," said Lance. "If Raina proves she can travel through time, they'll accept the rest of her story. That's the agreement. Since the time travel is the hard part."

"Ridiculous," I muttered. I went to the bathroom vanity and scooped cosmetics into a zippered pouch. I may have slammed a drawer or two. Behind me, I heard Meg saying, "Don't mind Zara. She gets like this sometimes."

I poked my head out of the bathroom to glare at Meg. "Thanks a lot. Like what?"

Meg grinned. "Like, in a swivet."

Lance's smile was sly. "She'll just get madder if we tell her how cute she is."

"And you don't want that," I said. "So knock it off."

Lance's voice sounded in my mind. *Why are you mad?*

Why are you not? I shot back. *This sucks. I thought we were done. I thought I was "in."*

The hard part's over. You passed the test. You just don't have your diploma yet.

For Meg's benefit, Lance switched back to the spoken word. "A quick trip to Washington won't be so bad," he said. He sent me an image of the two of us in the third row of that SUV, hour after hour. I had to admit, the idea had a certain appeal.

"It's not the trip," I said. "I was willing to make the trip. Get to know a few spellspinners, hear some stories from Rune, get acquainted with my mother, find out something about my roots." *Be with you.* I shut the suitcase. "All that is fine. What ticks me off is that I'm supposed to be a creature of power, and I never felt more powerless in my life. Go here, go there, do this, do that. I barely got home, and the same people who locked me in a tree cell, thank you very much, are whisking me away again."

"They're your people now," said Lance.

Bingo.

No wonder I was mad.

Chapter 13

I had to pack a couple of days' worth of stuff for Raina too, of course, because the woman had no twenty-first century clothes. Fortunately, my least-favorite outfits turned out to be her favorites. And she looked better in them than the mother of a sixteen year-old had any right to look. I might have been jealous of the way she looked in my clothes, if she hadn't been, you know, my *mother* – a concept I still had trouble wrapping my head around.

It was mid-afternoon by the time we got away, and autumn days are short. Nonny cast a long shadow in the slanting golden light, as she stood on the porch and waved goodbye. She looked small and forlorn. Her expression made me think she was regretting her decision to stay home and take care of her somewhat-neglected-lately nursery business, rather than go traipsing up to Washington with us.

Pearl sensed my thoughts. "It's for the best," she said. "It's easier this way."

Rune aimed a flicker of warning at Pearl. I felt it because Rune and I were touching. Much to our annoyance, Lance and I were separated. He was in the way-back, and I shared the middle seat with Rune on my right and Raina on my left. Beryl was driving and Pearl rode shotgun.

"What was that about?" I asked Rune. The time for secrets being, you know, past. "Was Pearl about to say too much? Are you guys planning to send arsonists in, when we're halfway to Washington, to burn down my home?"

"Of course not," said Rune. But the vibe was uncomfortable.

"What, then?"

Pearl yanked her visor down so her eyes could meet mine in the vanity mirror. "I only meant that the fewer sticks along for this ride, the better. Meaning no offense."

"None taken," said Raina.

"And?" I said.

Pearl sighed. "And if your Nonny'd come with us, we'd have to return to Cherry Glen to bring her back. Without her along for the ride, we don't have to. There. Are you satisfied? What a difficult child you are."

"As far as I'm concerned, you never have to return to Cherry Glen," I said.

"Neither do you," said Pearl. "Although you seem to want to. Doesn't matter. You're going to be away for a tad longer than you planned. For the next several months, you go where we go. And vice versa."

"Now, wait a minute—"

"Those were the terms," said Rune quietly. "We accept you. You accept us. You're under my protection now, and I'm responsible for teaching you. Remember?"

I shut my mouth and fumed. Lance's mind touched mine. *You wanted to learn, right? Stop fighting it.*

He was right. Everybody was right. I am a spellspinner. New rules apply, and I have to learn what they are. I *want* to learn what they are. I tried all summer to get Lance to teach me.

Of course, even then I fought it. I was like, teach me everything there is to know about being a spellspinner, but don't make me *be* one.

Was I wrong? I hate being wrong.

"Sorry," I said. It didn't sound sincere. I tried again. "Everything's moving too fast for me."

Raina's hand slipped inside my elbow and she gave my arm a squeeze. "It's hard," she said. "They will never understand how difficult it is. They've lived with it always. You are adjusting to a reality you never expected to face. A reality you never knew existed."

Her hazel eyes were warm with understanding. She knew. Of all the people who walked the earth—who ever walked the earth—I sat beside the one person who understood exactly what I was going through, in ways even Lance could not.

"Did it make you mad?" I asked. "For no particular reason?"

"For a very good reason. My life was ripped away from me in a flash. Every plan I had, everything I thought I knew, everyone I cared about, every familiar place—gone. I lashed out at everyone, even those who tried to help me."

"Why didn't you step into the wormhole? Try to get back?"

"By the time I understood what had happened to me, I was far away. And well guarded. Some thought I was in danger; some that I was dangerous. Either way, all agreed I must be held prisoner."

"Sounds familiar," I said wryly.

"It worked out for the best," she said, patting my hand. "I've no regrets. Apart from the obvious."

I didn't know what she meant. "Obvious?"

She nodded, hugged my arm again, and gazed out the window. I suddenly realized she wasn't answering because she couldn't speak.

Oh. She meant me.

Raina squared her shoulders and turned back to me, her hair slithering down to frame her face in a curtain of gleaming darkness. "I know now that you are the only child I shall have," she said, in a voice too soft for the others to hear. "And I missed your childhood."

"You're about to miss the rest of my life too," I pointed out. "Since you're going back to the seventeen hundreds."

She smiled a strange, fey smile and nodded. "That I am," she agreed. "But who's to say I won't come back?"

Interesting.

"Well, if you do, try to time it better," I said. "I don't think I could handle having my twenty-four year-old mother show up at my retirement party."

I let her hold my arm until we stopped for dinner. It seemed to comfort her. And although I have definitely reached the age where I'm not crazy about being cuddled by my mother, I was also aware that this would likely be my only chance to experience it. Better late than never.

There would be frost by morning. The air was so cold, we could see our breath steaming even in the near-dark. It wasn't completely dark. There was moonlight, the yellow bug light outside the office, and the flickering neon of Gus's sign: TREESIDE LODG . The final E was completely dark. Somehow it seemed appropriate.

Gus, it turned out, was the name of the owner/manager Lance had ripped off. And Rune, it turned out, was filthy rich and willing to smooth things over for his wayward nephew. And Lance, it turned out, knew how to deliver a handsome apology. So we were gracing the Treeside Lodge once again with our presence. Raina had faded out shortly after dinner and needed a good night's sleep. The rest of us thought a break and a hot shower sounded good; it wasn't like we had an appointment at the wormhole and needed to barrel up the road all night to make it. So here we were.

Lance and I had unfinished business — and paying Gus back was the small half of that. I had learned a few things on the ride up here.

We had (silently) agreed to meet on the hill behind the motel after everyone had settled in for the night. I was sharing a room with Raina, and Lance was in with Rune — as if that could keep us apart. Ha.

I arrived at our rendezvous before Lance did. Raina fell asleep the instant her head hit the pillow, which made it easy to slip out. Rune, I knew, was unlikely to sleep at all, but he never policed Lance anyway. So it was a sure bet Lance would arrive soon. I found a fallen log and sat, looking over the motel roof to the highway. It was cold and lonesome, and so was I.

I watched the occasional pair of headlights whoosh around the curve and vanish as if the forest were swallowing car after car. I needed this space to sit alone and gather my thoughts.

I was at a crossroads in my life. But I felt like I had been dragged to it against my will, and was now being shoved down a path not of my choosing. I would sit here for a minute and gaze at the various directions I could take. And make sure the path others had chosen for me was the same path I would choose, were I not forced.

"Spellspinner," I whispered, watching the puff of steam the word made. A word I had first encountered only last summer. It seemed a lifetime ago. Maybe because I'd been one all my life; I just hadn't known what to call it.

Path One: Deny what I was. Suppress the powers. Live a normal life. That's the path I had been following until I met Lance, and it was the life I'd always assumed I wanted. Now it occurred to me that I hadn't actually chosen that path. Nonny had chosen it for me years ago, and hustled me down it before I was old enough to choose.

Path Two: Embrace what I was. This was the path my kinsmen were dragging me down. If I followed this path, I would have to leave the familiar world I loved, and learn new ways. New rules. New places and people. New dangers.

I was familiar, at least, with the dangers of the first path. My life—and Nonny's too—had been governed by the fear of exposure. We hid from outsiders; we had few friends and hardly even saw our relatives.

Her relatives. It cost me a pang to remember, yet again, the unsettling and still-new information that her family wasn't mine.

Bottom line? I had to admit, the life I loved hadn't been perfect.

But the second path — the spellspinner path — was worse than unfamiliar. It seemed lonely and cruel. Spellspinner babies were born at Spellhaven, which seemed (to me) a ghastly prospect for both mother and child. And the children were reared, for the first ten years or so at least, up in that remote forest stronghold, taught by a succession of quasi-parental figures who were not, actually, their parents. The whole point of this peculiar system was to discourage little spellspinners from forming close personal ties. Which prepared them for life as a permanent loner — the only safe life, for a spellspinner out in the world.

Path Two was even lonelier than Path One, it seemed to me.

Was there a third path?

I heard Lance's boots crunching in the leaves. As he climbed the hill, he rose up out of the darkness like Batman arriving to save the day. Night. Whatever. Was he my Path Three? Or just a detour, pulling me away from where I really needed to go?

A night breeze ruffled his hair. He smiled, and I no longer cared whether he was a detour or not. I took the hand he offered and let him pull me to my feet. And then I stopped thinking for a while.

Eventually he murmured, "Your nose is cold."

I smiled against his neck. "Not as cold as it was." I leaned back against the circle of his arms and studied his face.

I didn't need light to know his expression was serious. "Neither one of us is as cold as we were."

He was right. I had warmed to him, and he to me. A learning experience for both of us. Not that the questions had all been answered—far from it.

I sighed. "You're distracting me."

"Good." He leaned in to distract me some more, but this time I pulled back.

"Wait a minute, rich boy."

"*Rich* boy?"

"Yeah. Explain to me why you keep taking that five-finger discount when you clearly don't need to."

He dropped his arms, disgusted, and shoved his hands in his pockets. "Zara, you can be such a buzzkill. Didn't you play 'cops and robbers' when you were a kid?"

"No," I said.

"Oh yeah, I forgot. You didn't play anything. You didn't have friends."

"And you did? I thought you were raised in the forest like Mowgli, eating roots and berries and learning the ways of the pack. Which reminds me. Who are your parents?"

"It doesn't matter. I barely know them."

"On purpose. Yeah, I get that. But it does matter. I never met any group of people so obsessed with bloodlines."

"Okay, okay." He shot me a mental image of his parents.

I recognized them, but only as faces in the spellspinner crowd. And they had not been sitting together at the Spellhaven court or the Chapmans' barn. I could not remember any sign of affection, or greeting, passing between Lance and either one of them. Surprise held me speechless for a moment. "You're closer to Rune than you are to them."

"He's my guardian."

"Can't a parent be a guardian?"

Lance shook his head. "Too risky. Come on, Zara. You know this. The parent-child bond is dangerous, especially for the parent. A spellspinner's first, and only, authority is the Council. It has to be that way, for our own safety. What would have happened at Spellhaven if my mother had been allowed to form a maternal bond with me? Don't you think she would have tried to defy the Council? Rescue me? Intervene?" He shrugged. "Rune's attempts to influence the outcome raised a few eyebrows, but that was probably nothing compared to what my father would have done. If he were my father the way sticks have fathers."

I hugged myself, shivering. "That's just...sad."

"No, it's different. Not sad. Just different. You didn't have parents either."

"I had Nonny." A smile tugged at the corners of my mouth. "She'd go after the Council with a baseball bat if she had to, to protect me. Every kid should have someone who cares that much."

He took my hand. "Let's go sit in the car."

We headed downhill, the light link of our fingers bridging our minds as skin-to-skin contact always does. Halfway down we halted in our tracks, startled by a strange prickle at the backs of our necks. It was gone almost as soon as we sensed it.

What was that?

Lance pulled me to his side, his arm around my waist in a protective gesture. We stayed motionless for a few seconds, scenting the air like wary woodland animals. Whatever it was, it was gone now. But the car sounded like an even better idea.

Before following me into the back seat, Lance scanned the area again, frowning.

"Don't be paranoid." I grabbed his sleeve and hauled him in after me, laughing. "Careful is healthy. Paranoid is sick."

He slid in and slammed the door shut. Immediately the world hushed and we were enclosed in a cushioned leather cocoon. He flicked the air with his power and the air warmed. "Nice," I murmured. I waved my hand at the plushness surrounding us. "Smells like money to me, rich boy."

"Not my money. Rune's."

Rune, I had learned that afternoon, was a sculptor. He was an international marvel; Rune Donovan could do things with marble and granite that other people just couldn't do. (Duh.) He had created public art installations in major cities around the world, and even his smaller pieces sold for tons of money. Rune would probably have been an artist even if he weren't a spellspinner, but his enhanced ability to bend rock to his will gave him mad skills. So he was the rarest of rare birds: a wealthy artist.

And he was Lance's guardian. So there was no need, no need at all, for Lance to live on the edge the way he does.

"All I'm saying is—"

Lance's cool, strong fingers touched my lips, stopping my words. "I know what you're saying," he murmured. His green eyes gleamed in the near-dark. "Say it later."

His mouth came down on mine and my thoughts scattered and swooped away like a flock of startled birds.

Wholesoul intensified the kiss to an almost unbearable sweetness. I sank into his arms and surrendered to the dream, knowing that people all over the world spend their lives searching for a connection like this and most of them never find it. We floated together in a drugged and blissful oblivion, where it no longer mattered that I thought Lance was a cold-blooded sociopath and he thought I was a prissy little killjoy. Those were surface judgments, based on behaviors we could change if we chose. Underneath, in the most secret and powerful core of our beings, we were one, and always would be.

When we came up for air, the windows had steamed over.

Lance's mood turned serious. He threaded his fingers through my hair and cradled my head, studying my face. "It's over," he said. "And we both know it now."

A chill ran down my spine. "What's over?"

"The fighting. The big struggle." His fingertips traced my eyebrows. I closed my eyes. "It's you and me, Zara," he whispered. "Forever."

I couldn't help smiling a little. "You think we'll stop fighting?"

A silent laugh rocked his body. "Arguing isn't fighting."

"If you say so." I opened my eyes. Lance's face loomed above mine, so handsome it made my head swim. There was enough light from the motel's neon sign to read his expression, but I didn't need to read his expression to know how he felt. The depth of his devotion was humbling. And then I realized the cause. "I get it," I exclaimed. "You love me because I'm the other half of you."

He caught my hand mid-air as it was forming a fist. His face lit with laughter. "I might love you anyway."

"I bet you wouldn't," I growled. "Lance will always love Lance best." But I wasn't really mad. Because I understood him. And also because, whatever the source, he was, in fact, utterly, unshakably, sincerely committed to me. Which was gratifying.

His eyes searched mine, serious again. "It's more than that, and you know it. What I feel for you is…"

His voice trailed off as he searched for words. There was such oneness between us that I followed his search, sensing every nuance of emotion as he thumbed through his feelings like a deck of cards. He felt a lot for me. A lot. And most of it had nothing to do with me being the other half of him.

I tried not to smile. Failed. Beamed at him like the besotted fangirl I secretly had been for weeks. "Okay, I admit it. I confess. You got me. I'm nuts about you too."

It's hard to kiss someone who's smiling, but we both managed it. And it's amazing how quickly smiles can melt into something warmer and softer. *Oh, Lance.* It was a relief to not fight it anymore. Joy met hunger and fused into passion. We kissed and clung and whispered like a couple of lovesick honeymooners, for probably the happiest twenty minutes of my life so far. But I sensed there was still something Lance thought we should talk about, so eventually, with a sigh, I left his mouth and crawled back on his chest.

"What," I said, stupidly kissing his shirt.

"Our problem isn't us anymore," he said. "It's the Council."

"I'm sick of the Council." I lifted my face back to his, but he placed his fingers gently against my lips.

"I'm sick of them too, but they're not going anywhere. Gonna have to deal with them someday, babe."

I gave up and sat up. "Okay, I'll bite. How are they a problem?"

"Zara, I've pledged to obey them. But you're my priority now." His expression was troubled. "This is why our people fear wholesoul. It's why I wanted us to keep it secret as long as we could. Spellspinners with wholesoul are dangerous."

"But we don't want to hurt anybody. We're not going to start the next spellspinner wars. All we want is to be left alone."

"Remember: *All who will not join must die.* Will you join?"

"Of course I'll join." But uneasiness colored my words with hesitation, and Lance felt it. "If you can do it, I can do it," I said stubbornly.

"That's just it. I don't think I can do it anymore." He pulled me into his arms. I went willingly, and we rested against the door with Lance's head against the window and me snuggled into his chest. I could hear his heartbeat.

"Is that bad?" I asked, in a small voice. "People can be loyal to more than one thing. We can stand with the others. Maybe we'll never have to choose. Maybe they'll never ask us to do something we don't want to do."

He gave a derisive snort. "Yeah, they will. Like, if you ever have a child, they'll expect you to give it up. It will be raised at Spellhaven by people you barely know. I'm thinking you might have a problem with that."

"But that's a long way off," I said, hoping I was right. "Anything could happen between now and then. We'll have lots of time to convince them — "

I was interrupted by a loud bang, as if someone had set off a firecracker just outside the car. I jumped and screamed; a complete reflex.

Lance, however, didn't move.

I was instantly plunged into a haze of equal parts panic and confusion, enhanced by a loud ringing in my ears as my hearing tried to recover from the explosion. I watched, as if in a dream, as Lance slipped sideways, leaving a smear of blood against the window behind his head. A neat, round hole in the glass slid into view as he fell.

"Lance!" I screamed, stupidly. And then: "No! No! No!"

My head and shoulders whacked painfully against the ceiling as I tried to jump up, forgetting that I was inside the SUV. Then I was out of the car, I don't know how, stumbling across the gravel and screaming for help.

I knew who had done it. I knew it in my bones. I looked around wildly, but saw nothing; no movement; there was no flash of auburn hair or click of high-heeled boots. A small, pearl-handled pistol lay in the gravel beside the car as if tossed away.

Of course, I thought numbly. Of course she's not here now. She skatched. It used to be the only power she was really good at. But apparently, with fewer spellspinners walking the planet, even Amber's powers increased. She had followed us, and we never even knew it.

Lights were switching on inside motel rooms. Curtains twitched. One or two people peered out through their windows. A couple of doors opened. One of the doors that opened was Rune's, and that's all I cared about. He was still completely dressed. An open book dropped from his fingers as he sized up the situation. Then he sprinted toward me, shouting over his shoulder for Beryl.

I grabbed Rune's arm and dragged him to the car. "She shot him," I sobbed. "She shot Lance."

"Who?"

"Who do you *think?*"

Rune wrenched the door open. Lance's body slid bonelessly into his arms. There was blood, a lot of it. "Dear God," whispered Rune. I could feel his horror, beating through the air in thick waves of emotion. I couldn't speak anymore. I'd been paralyzed by a question too monstrous to ask. I sagged against the car, shaking, unable to take my eyes from Lance's still, white face.

Rune shouted over his shoulder. "Beryl!"

"I'm here," she said. She was striding across the parking lot in her bare feet, enveloped in a huge corduroy bathrobe that made her look like a sailing ship. She crouched beside Rune and placed her palms on Lance's forehead. "Whuff," she grunted. "That's bad."

"He's breathing," said Rune. Which meant that I could breathe again, too.

"Give me his head," said Beryl.

Pearl arrived, hair askew, wearing pink sweats and fuzzy slippers that crunched against the gravel as she trotted up. "Drat the child," she said, irritated. I knew that, for once, she didn't mean me. "What's she done now?"

"Keep back," warned Beryl. "He's been shot in the back of the neck. Bullet's still there. Must've been a pipsqueak of a gun."

Pearl was startled. "She *shot* him? Shot Lance?" Her eyes went to me. Clearly she assumed Amber's aim was bad.

Gus hurried toward us, yanking overall straps over his pajamas as he ran. "Holy cow," he said. "Holy cow. Should I call 911?"

"No need," said Beryl calmly. She was cradling Lance's head in her arms. "It's not as bad as it looks." Everyone but Gus knew she was lying.

Gus's eyebrows rose. "Looks bad enough. Holy cow. What happened?"

"Jilted girlfriend," said Rune. "Came back to make a point."

He rose and turned to engage Gus in conversation, cleverly blocking the old man's view. Gus seemed torn between an impulse to call the cops, and a desire to minimize everything. It was his property, after all, and nobody wants their motel in the news as a crime scene. Rune was handling him well, which was a relief. I had to concentrate on Lance. Pearl joined Rune and Gus, casually covering the discarded gun with one of her fuzzy slippers.

I sat in the dirt next to Beryl and took Lance's hand in mine. It was frightening to touch him and feel nothing there. I sent my senses into him, searching desperately for a flicker, for a whiff, of Lance-ness. No answering spirit met mine.

Terror grabbed me by the throat and shook me. Was he gone? It was unthinkable. It was literally unthinkable. My mind shrank back from the possibility, curled in on itself, and refused to go there.

It was impossible, it must be impossible, for Lance to die.

This kind of thing only happens to other people. You hear about it on the news all the time—lives snuffed out in an instant—but it never happens to anyone you know. It couldn't have happened to Lance, of all people. He was just here. He was warm and living, in my arms, telling me he loved me, five minutes ago.

How could I face life without Lance? If I even pictured it for a second, I would go stark, staring mad.

No, I mustn't think it—I mustn't think it—my hands were already shaking. They couldn't shake. *Focus, Zara!* I screamed inside my head. *What if he needs you?*

I forced myself to breathe. I forced myself to concentrate. I placed one hand on his forehead.

Lance, I cried silently. *Where are you?*

I did not feel Lance. What I did feel, surprisingly, was Beryl. I picked up a strong sense of her, her mind intensely concentrated on Lance's injuries, probing without touching, seeing with her eyes closed. Through her mind I understood the nature of splintered bone and mangled flesh, and perceived the bullet, an alien lump of metal lodged against C4.

Beryl's vocabulary gifted me with what to call it. It was one of the little bones in Lance's neck, and if he'd been a stick the shot might have killed or paralyzed him. Spellspinners are tough, but apparently if you shoot one in the neck you can do some damage. Just not as much damage as you intended.

At least not when Beryl is around.

I witnessed it myself or I might not have believed it. She used telekinesis to remove the bullet. She worked it carefully out with her mind, sliding it backwards through the very path it had made on its way in. And as it went, she used her powers to seal Lance's flesh behind it, or at least align the muscles, tendons and bones so they would heal with maximum efficiency. When the bullet fell into her palm I stared at her. "That's amazing."

She was still focused on Lance, but she shot me a quick, amused glance. "Hush. You'll blow our cover." With her hands still cradling Lance, being careful not to jostle him,

Beryl called to Rune. "There are first aid supplies in the back end. Can you open the lift gate without rocking the car?"

"You bet," said Rune, moving swiftly behind his formerly-gorgeous SUV. The back door lifted without rocking the car at all. If Gus hadn't been so distracted, he might have wondered how Rune managed that. Similarly, the car didn't move while Rune rummaged through the bits of luggage that we'd left in the back when we checked in, and unearthed Beryl's box of medical supplies. Poor old Gus was as oblivious to Rune's magic as Lance was, but I noticed, and was grateful.

I steadied Lance while Beryl staunched the wound, cleaned him up a bit, and immobilized his head and neck by strapping him into a contraption made out of plastic and foam. Rune somehow convinced Gus there was nothing for him to do, so he could go back to bed—thank goodness. So, freed from observation, the four of us glided Lance up to the room he was sharing with Rune and laid him on his bed as smoothly as if he were floating on a cushion of warm air. Which he was, thanks to Beryl's direction and our combined powers.

"Step up, Little Miss Wholesoul," said Beryl, gesturing at Lance's still form. "You can probably help him more than I can, now."

No point in demurring. It was obvious they all knew what Lance and I had.

I sat on the bed and placed one hand lightly on Lance's forehead again, taking his hand with my other hand. And this time, I felt his presence. Relief flooded me.

He was still unconscious, but he was there. He seemed to me...because he seemed, to himself...to be lying at the bottom of a well, staring at a pool of light far above his head. Darkness beat at the edges of his mind, pulling him first farther away, then closer, then away again.

"Lance," I whispered. "Come on. We're up here."

He wasn't dying. I knew this because I sensed that the pool of light held *this* world, not any world beyond. It was this world that hovered above him, out of reach. It was this world he was struggling to reach. It was me.

Me, and everything else—but mostly me. The other half of his soul.

I reached down the well. He reached up.

About halfway to the surface, the pain kicked in. We were so fused, we both felt it. I sent a fierce blast of power against it, but killing pain is not my area of expertise. Lance's will is strong, however, and he dealt with it better than I did. Instead of fighting it, he ignored it. A few seconds later there was movement behind his eyelids and his breathing changed.

Beryl exclaimed, "He's coming around. Good job." She took over, easing his pain by blocking the nerve signals or something; I picked up the general sense of it but I'm not sure exactly what she did. Anyway, it worked. Lance's green, green eyes opened. "Don't try to move," she warned him.

"I promise," he muttered. And closed his eyes again.

"You'll be good as new in a day or two," she said. "The faintness you're feeling is from blood loss."

I stared at her. "A day or two? That's all?"

"Thanks to Beryl," said Pearl. "We heal quickly, but she's able to line things up so they heal right. It's her gift."

"What's yours?" I asked, curious now.

She gave a quick snort of laughter. "Growin' cranberries."

"She's got other gifts," said Beryl. "But she does run a mean cranberry bog."

"It's a living," said Pearl. "If you're wondering where Rune went, he took off for Spellhaven. Unlikely that Amber's gone there, although she might have. Lord knows the child's not thinking straight. But he'll summon the rest of the Council and report what happened."

"If he's summoning the Council, won't you have to go?"

"Once it's time to decide, I will. Right now my task is to bring them the rest of the story." She jerked her chin at Lance. "I hope to be able to report no harm was done."

Anger whipped through me. "She could have killed him."

Pearl nodded. "Or you, for that matter. But she didn't."

I was speechless.

Beryl snorted. "She didn't, because Rune had the foresight to include me in your little jaunt. You going to give Amber a pass, Pearl? Your bias is showing."

Pearl sighed. "All right. Guilty. You're right." She slumped in the ratty little chair in the corner of the room. "She was such a cute little thing when she was four. Hard to believe she's gone feral."

Beryl's mouth tightened. "It happens." She glanced at me. "One of the drawbacks of how we're raised, if you ask me. Seems we have more than our share of sociopaths."

There was a soft tap on the door. We froze.

"It's me," said Raina's voice outside.

Pearl sighed again, then left her chair for a moment and opened the door. Raina's eyes were heavy with sleep, but she looked like a million bucks in my wine velvet Christmas bathrobe. "What's going on?" She moved to Lance's bedside, taking it all in. Her gaze was fastened on Lance with a suitably horrified expression, but her hands reached for me, stroking my hair in a soothing, motherly way, as if I were the one needing comfort.

Where did she learn that? Must be instinct. Whatever it was, I hadn't realized I needed it until she gave it to me. Then I was suddenly blinking back tears. I moved away, unsettled by my reaction to Raina's way-too-late mothering.

"He'll be fine," said Beryl. "But Amber shot him."

Raina's hand fluttered up to cover her mouth. Her eyes were wide with shock.

"Yeah," I said. "Rune's gone to tell the Council."

"He's gone to Spellhaven," said Raina. It wasn't a question.

Pearl shifted uncomfortably in her chair. "The sooner we get you back to the 1700s, the better," she grumbled. "Gives me the fidgets to hear a stick talk about Spellhaven."

"What a thing to say." Raina looked annoyed. "Whose idea do you think it was? Spellhaven, I mean."

We all looked at her. I even felt a glimmer of surprise come from Lance's half-dreaming brain.

She raked her hair back from her face and straightened her spine. "Now, really," she chided. "Use your heads. How would a band of early eighteenth-century Celts know about the redwood forests of the Pacific Northwest?"

Pearl and Beryl looked thunderstruck. It had clearly never occurred to them to ask that glaringly obvious question.

Laughter rose up in my throat and forced itself out in a kind of choked guffaw. I couldn't help it. Maybe there was a hysterical edge to it, but it still felt good to laugh. I collapsed onto Rune's bed, laughing until I could scarcely breathe.

My father ended the spellspinner wars and formed the first Council. My mother basically invented Spellhaven. And everyone, including me, had been wringing their hands over whether or not I was a spellspinner? I was the most spellspinnerish spellspinner that had ever lived. I was, like, spellspinner royalty.

The irony was just killingly funny.

Chapter 14

I caught a whiff of fresh rain and the sharp fragrance of redwoods, and when I turned around Rune was there, brushing raindrops off his coat. He nodded a greeting at Raina, but his focus was on Lance.

"How's the patient?" he asked, keeping his voice low.

"Recruiting his strength," said Beryl. "He'll be fine soon enough."

Rune sighed. "That's one good thing." His expression was grim.

My heart sank. "What happened?"

"Not much. Amber wasn't there. We set a guard over her skatching stone, but—" He shrugged. "She's unlikely to use it."

Raina was puzzled. "Why did you think Amber might be at Spellhaven? I should think it would be the last place she'd go, after doing a thing like this."

"Spellspinners are born at Spellhaven now," I told her. "Supposedly the place where you're born is the easiest place to skatch to, in moments of danger or stress. We imprint. Like baby ducks."

Rune frowned. "Well, not quite."

"Close enough. Anyway, that's why we thought Amber might be there. But she wasn't."

"Did you try her house?" asked Pearl.

"Not there either," said Rune. "Opal's keeping an eye on it."

Pearl snorted. "Opal Donovan is a nincompoop."

"Maybe, but she's the only one of us who's been to Amber's house, so it had to be Opal. We're sending the

Pearce boys down from Boston, but it's a bit of a ride to South Carolina even from there, let alone from here."

We all looked at each other as the realization sank in that Amber was on the run, and probably the only way we'd ever find her was pure dumb luck. Rune sat on his bed and rubbed his face tiredly. "Not good," he muttered. "This is not good at all."

Raina's arm went around me in a protective gesture. "Are you telling me that my Zara has to spend the rest of her life looking over her shoulder?" Her voice was sharper than I'd ever heard it. "I want this girl found. Now. You're all supposed to have powers! Use them."

"We're not detectives," said Pearl testily. "What good are powers like ours in a case like this? Amber has 'em too. She sees us coming, she disappears."

"If you can't use your powers, use your heads," snapped Raina. "You know her, I don't. Where would she go? What would she do?"

In the brief silence that followed, we all bent our minds to the problem. It seemed to me that Amber was not only unhinged, she had never been bright to begin with, and her powers were weak — for a spellspinner. She was impulsive. Driven by emotion. She relied on her looks so much that she was out of practice in tackling problems with her brain. So where would she go?

Somewhere she'd been before, obviously, since she'd skatched to get there. Probably a place she'd been to fairly recently. Something dramatic had happened in this place, something that had imprinted itself on her internal skatching GPS. The Chapmans' barn?

No. It would also be a place the Council didn't know about. Somewhere no Council member had ever been, so no authority figures could follow her there.

And suddenly I knew exactly where she'd gone.

The only question was, was Amber stupid enough to still be there?

If she thought she'd shot me instead of Lance, my bet was yes. She'd still be there, waiting for Lance to realize where she'd gone, and come to her.

What a dope. Because if she *had* shot me, and Lance *did* come to her, he'd do exactly what I was about to do.

I took a deep breath and straightened my spine. "Okay," I said.

Rune's aquamarine eyes glittered as his gaze locked with mine. He had picked up some inkling of my thoughts. "What are you doing? Don't you dare—"

"You set guards on Amber's skatching stone, right?"

"Yes, but—"

"You should go back there and join them, just in case. I have an idea." And I skatched.

☆

A cold wind sent fallen leaves scuttling across the pavement like frightened crabs and tossed the empty branches above my head as if the trees surrounding me were wringing their hands in distress. It was dark, but I had my power stone. Night-blindness did not afflict me. I knew exactly where I was, and every inch of the cement path beneath my feet was familiar. Faint light from the globe of an old-fashioned streetlight on the corner glimmered on the gazebo's white paint straight ahead. I jammed my hands in my pockets and strode toward it, righteous anger propelling me to where I knew she'd be.

Amber was huddled on the gazebo steps, hugging her knees. I'd never seen her look miserable. It startled me. She lifted her face to stare at mine. Her eyes were dull with pain and her cheeks were wet with tears, but her expression conveyed no emotion at all. "You," she said.

"That's right," I said pleasantly. "Next time, aim before you shoot."

The force of Amber's body hitting mine knocked the breath right out of me. She had skatched right *into* me, fast as a lightning strike — and with much the same effect. I saw stars.

Should I have anticipated this? Yes, I should have. Later, if I survived, I would curse myself for an idiot. At the moment, blinded and winded, I hit the ground. Immediately she was on top of me, grabbing my hair and twisting, immobilizing my head. She gave a mighty heave and rolled us sideways.

The last time she tried this trick, I had ended up with my back pressed against the earth, and the earth is where our power comes from. It had been child's play to defeat her. This time, she made sure she was on the ground, from shoulder to heel, and I was disadvantaged. It took me half a heartbeat to figure out why. She had rolled me onto the cement path. Amber had the sweet clean lawn against her body. I had a layer of concrete dulling my connection to the planet.

Strong hands closed around my throat, slim fingers digging painfully into my flesh, cutting off my air and the blood flow to my brain. In seconds I would be unconscious.

Oh, Amber. Silly girl. The last time you tried to take me out, I did not yet know what I was.

With just the tiniest push of power, my throat turned hard as marble. It no longer mattered that her hands were supernaturally strong. My neck was supernaturally stronger. Breath and blood flowed once more and the stars that had spun across my vision returned to their proper place in the sky.

I sensed a flicker of uncertainty as Amber felt the change beneath her fingers, and that was all the opening I needed. I slammed my power into her body and sent her flying.

I hadn't meant to hurt her, but we were in a park. She shot backwards across the grass like a hockey puck on ice, and whammed into a tree trunk. I leapt to my feet and let the power pour through me, healing me, protecting me, and filling me with fire. I saw myself through Amber's eyes. Her mind was open to me now, like a cracked egg, spilling every secret. I felt her fury. Her humiliation. And her fear. I looked like an avenging goddess. My eyes were glowing like purple lamps, my hair writhed like a living thing, and sparks of pale amethyst haloed my entire body.

I pointed at her. Sparks streamed from my fingertip and surrounded Amber in a cloud of shimmering purple light. She was imprisoned in a cocoon of my power. I felt her trying to skatch. I smiled. She could no more skatch than a stick could. Not now. Not while I held her captive.

"Get up," I said. My voice thrummed with Power. Amber slowly got to her feet. I was still pointing at her. I raised my arm slightly and she rose into the air. I dangled her there, about three feet off the ground, just to demonstrate what she was up against.

"I could snuff out your life like a candle," I said. "I could cripple you. I could blind you. I could put a glamour on you that you couldn't break, one that makes everyone who sees you think you are covered with warts or pimples or oozing sores. But I'm going to do none of those things, Amber. I want you to remember that. I want you to remember all the things I might have done to you, and didn't. I am not going to hurt you. I'm just going to make sure you can't hurt me. Bye-bye."

I pulled, and up from the ground came Power, shooting through the soles of my feet and all the way through me, out my fingertip and into Amber.

She vanished. I smiled.

I knew where she had gone, because Lance told me where he went when I banished him. She was at Spellhaven now, and the spellspinners guarding her skatching stone had her.

Amber would never again come within a hundred miles of me. I would see her at Spellhaven when I went there, no doubt, but she'd be harmless. I'd defanged the snake. Any attempt to do me harm would hurt her more than it hurt me. She was banished, and far more thoroughly than Lance had been. I had my power stone now.

I sent the Power back into the earth. My hair fell back into place, tumbling past my shoulders in its normal way. The sparkly purple light shimmered away into nothingness, and I stood in the darkness of Cherry Glen's deserted town square, breathing the cold, damp cleanness of an autumn night. I smiled, and stretched, and sighed. It felt good.

Chapter 15

Pearl opened the door. Raina cried out with relief and rushed to hug me, but I could feel Lance's anger pounding at me the instant I stepped into the room. Rune was nowhere to be seen.

"Rune's at Spellhaven?" I asked. It was hard to speak through the choking blanket of Lance's anger.

Pearl's sharp eyes went from me to Lance, then back to me. She sensed the vibe—although it wasn't affecting her, of course. "Yep, he went back, the minute you left. Care to tell us what's going on?"

First things first. I pulled away from Raina and joined Beryl at Lance's bedside. He was sitting up already. Anger must be good for him. "New rule," he said. "Zara doesn't skatch without consulting Lance."

I had been about to apologize, but, as usual, he ticked me off before I had a chance to start.

I scowled. "What if I'm drowning?"

"If you're talking about that little jaunt you made to Camp Greenhorn, you wouldn't have been there if you'd listened to me. But no, you just *went,* without even thinking it through, let alone consulting me, or even Nonny—"

"Ask a stick before I skatch? Boy, I never thought I'd hear that advice from you, of all people—"

"Even a stick knows you should look before you leap."

"Yeah, right. Except you can't look until you leap."

Lance's green eyes glittered. "I want you safe. You got a problem with that?"

Beryl's mild voice cut in before we really started to fight. "Skatching blind is only for emergencies."

I snorted and jammed my hands in my pockets. "Everybody knows that."

A brief silence fell while they all looked at me. Defeated, I sank onto the edge of Rune's bed. "My life is full of emergencies," I muttered.

"Tell us about this latest one," said Pearl. "Lance thought you went back to Cherry Glen. Did you find Amber?"

"Right where I thought she'd be."

"And?" Pearl's voice sounded strained. I looked at her in surprise, and then at Beryl, for the first time getting past my own emotions—and Lance's— to sense the dread and sadness emanating from the older ladies.

"Good grief, did you think I'd hurt her? I just kinda boxed her up and shipped her to Spellhaven. Let the Council deal with her. That's the spellspinner way, right?"

In the end, that was what saved us. I guess you can swear till you're blue in the face that you don't mean any harm, but nobody will really trust you unless and until you prove it somehow. If my newfound kin knew anything about me, it was that I am (a) powerful and (b) impulsive. This can be a dangerous combination. I get that. But my actions when the chips were down, so to speak, revealed something about my nature that eased their minds a bit.

My first, unfiltered instinct was not to take revenge on someone who had harmed and angered me, but rather to defer to the Council's judgment.

When I had Amber completely at my mercy, mercy was what she got.

Had I thought about it ahead of time? No. Was I playing politics, sparing her life because I knew it would look good to the Council? Not hardly. It was obvious to one and all that I didn't think before I acted, because, to be perfectly honest, impulsiveness is probably my biggest fault.

And for once, that turned out to be a good thing. Zara uncensored, as it were, turned out to have pretty good instincts.

Lance razzed me about it, but I know he was just as relieved as I was. A day will probably come when we defy the Council, but for now, we're golden.

As soon as we were out of sight of Gus's motel, Beryl pulled the SUV off the road and we all got out. Rune touched it with his sculptor's hands. The shattered window knitted itself back together; the bloodstains dissolved and vanished; the dent my hard head had made in the ceiling smoothed out, and the vehicle was good as new.

"Well, that's that," said Pearl, in a voice of satisfaction. "No lasting damage after all."

Beryl cut her a sideways glance. "You got to watch that soft spot you have for Amber Carrick."

Pearl looked defensive. "I wasn't saying anything. I've a soft spot for Zara too, in case you didn't notice."

"All I did was banish her," I reminded them. "It keeps her away from me, not anybody else. As far as I'm concerned, she can live long and prosper. Just not where I am. You don't have to feel sorry for poor little Amber."

"Hey, what about me?" said Lance. "I'm the one she shot."

His arm was around me, so I bumped him with my hip. "Stick with me and you'll be fine."

"What am I, your prisoner?"

"Is that so bad?"

His green eyes gleamed. "Ask me in a decade or two."

"Get in the car," said Rune dryly. "We all have to be present for Amber's trial. Lance can put his own whammy on her when he sees her at Spellhaven."

"Darn," I said. "I kinda liked the prisoner idea."

We got in the car.

We spent a night in Portland, Oregon, and then spent the whole next day getting to Merlin, Washington. It wasn't a gazillion miles from Portland, it was just that the roads were slow. Really slow. We twisted and bumped and crawled through what seemed an unending, mountainous forest, and it rained so hard that a lot of the time we could barely see the road. The only good part was, they let me and Lance sit together in the way-back. So even though we were probably jolted harder than anybody else in the SUV, we didn't much care.

Turns out I was born in Merlin, in the only hospital for miles around. If you've never been to Merlin, don't worry about it. You haven't missed much.

There are two motels in town, an EconoLodge and a Good Nite Inn. I guess they do a booming business housing folks whose loved ones are in the hospital. Lord knows there's nothing else to bring people to Merlin. We chose the Good Nite Inn. Rune and Pearl grumbled about spending yet another night in a cheap room, but Raina just laughed. "It has plumbing," she reminded them. "How bad could it be?"

"My uncle's a snob," said Lance.

"And I'm a cranky old woman," said Pearl. "A cranky old twenty-first century woman. Plumbing! Ha. Electricity too, no doubt. Guess I should count my blessings."

"As should we all," said Raina. She was cheerful as a sparrow in spring. I don't know why she was in such a good mood. Maybe it was the removal of the threat to her only child's safety. Or, possibly, the prospect of ditching said child and vanishing back to the seventeen hundreds. At any rate, the woman was glowing with happiness. "Do you suppose there's a sporting goods store around here someplace?"

I stared at her blankly, picturing sleeping bags, baseball mitts, and fishing poles. "What for?"

She blushed. "I have a little money. I'd like to pick up a couple of things for the…for the journey."

"Let's check in first," said Beryl. "I'm dying to stretch my legs."

I was burning with curiosity, but had to hold my horses until we were done with the logistics of room-buying and luggage-toting.

Lance politely carried Raina's and my bags to our little double-bedded room and tossed them on the fold-out suitcase racks. "Sporting goods," he reminded Raina. "Why?"

She bit her lip. "Well, Helga gave me some cash in case I needed it. Or in case Zara needed it. But Rune has paid for everything so far. So if Zara doesn't mind – "

"I won't mind."

"I'd like to take a couple of modern conveniences back with me."

I was surprised, to say the least. "You can do that?"

She nodded. "Within reason. Whatever is in my pockets travels with me. The first time I went, I wasn't expecting it, of course, so only my clothes and shoes went with me. And the plastic comb I had in my pocket—a marvel to all who behold it." She chuckled. "When I came back here to have my baby, I wore a silver brooch. I sold it to a nice lady in the maternity ward, but not for much. I don't think she believed me when I told her how old it was."

"What did you buy then, to take back to the seventeen hundreds?" I asked.

"Two boxes of ball-point pens, some toothbrushes, and a solar calculator."

"Wow."

"You'd be surprised, the things you miss." Raina rummaged briefly in our combined luggage, and pulled out her kirtle, shaking out the folds. "This time, I came prepared." She pointed proudly to the pockets sewn in each side of the skirt. "I brought plenty of things I could sell, and gifts for Helga, because I was determined to find her. And through her, you. I never dreamed she actually kept you, and that when I found her, I'd find you too. That's been the only easy part of this adventure." She smiled. "So don't be thinking I'm robbing your Nonny. I gave her some highly valuable antiques, including an Irish illuminated manuscript—small, but possibly worth more than all the jewelry put together. I also brought this." She pulled out a square of pink paper and tenderly unfolded it. "I carry it with me always," she whispered. "But you should have it."

I held it up to the light, puzzled. It was old-fashioned NCR paper, the kind that creates multiple copies when you write on the top sheet. This was the back sheet, so the carbon-y ink had faded and blurred. Across the bottom was stamped "Patient copy."

It was my birth record. I got gooseflesh thinking she had filled it out right there in the hospital across the street, the doctor had signed it, and she'd carried it with her through the centuries and back.

Lance leaned over my shoulder. "Cool," he said reverently.

"Epic cool," I murmured. "Check it out, Donovan. I exist."

"I was pretty sure you did."

"Yeah, but now we know for sure." I pointed at the center of the sheet, half disappointed. "No middle name. Just Zara."

My mother looked amused. "Don't forget, I had to embroider it on your baby blanket. The fewer letters, the better."

"Right. I'm lucky you didn't name me X."

"Believe me, I was tempted."

We all laughed, but the sadness in Raina's eyes was unmistakable. It was costing her something, to give away this cherished bit of paper—even to me.

Lance picked up my thought and snapped his fingers. "Idea." He pulled his phone out of his pocket. Mine was still at the police station back in Cherry Glen. "I have a scanning app."

"Brilliant," I said, and meant it. Raina looked confused. I held up the birth record. "We can both have it," I told her. "Lance will take a picture of it, and I can use that to order a certified copy of the original. You know, in case I ever want to drive a car or vote or something. And you can keep this one."

So the next morning, when Raina took her last hot shower and donned her antique outfit, my birth record was tucked in the bottom of one of her pockets. "For luck," she said, patting it.

The day had dawned pearly and damp, but the rain had stopped and the sun was making an effort to show. We crawled down what Raina called "the highway," a two-lane road that snaked through — what else? — dense forest. We saw hardly any other cars. Raina sat beside me, her body taut with tension as she scanned the side of the road.

We were nearly an hour out of town when she saw it. "There," she said, pointing. "Stop."

Beryl found a piece of shoulder that didn't seem too awfully muddy, and pulled over. We climbed out. Raina barely glanced at any of us; all her focus was elsewhere now. She was like an arrow quivering on a string, waiting to be loosed. It made me sad to see her so keen to leave this century. I tried to keep a lid on it. I knew my reaction was selfish.

Raina's looped her train through her belt, cinched it tight, and ran lightly back down the road, flitting like a ghost in the mist rising from the ground. She stopped by a tree that looked exactly like all the other trees to me, and ran her fingers over the marks she'd made: three broken branches and some peeled bark. "This is it," she said happily.

The forest looked impenetrable. The trees grew thick and close, the ground blocked with fallen logs and dense thickets of fern. And the land sloped upward. And everything was wet.

I peered glumly into the dimness. "How deep do we have to go?"

"Not far," said Raina. "Probably less than a mile."

"A mile," said Pearl. "Through that? Hmf. Think I'll wait in the car with Beryl."

Rune zipped his jacket. "Well, I have to go in," he said. "I'm the Council's witness."

I patted Raina's sleeve. "Sure you don't want to rethink this? Stick around for a while?"

She was barely tethered to the ground, she was so eager to go. "I dare not," she said. "When I birthed you I was away for a few days only, yet when I returned five years had passed."

Even the cadence of her speech was dialing back toward my father's time.

So, into the woods we went. Lance and Rune took turns carrying the box of modern goodies Raina had bought to take into the wormhole. It was rough going, but not as rough as I had expected. The canopy of trees was so dense that the ground was, for the most part, damp rather than soaked. Raina led the way, her skirts seeming to impede her very little. I wasn't able to look up from my feet often to admire her skill, but when I did, I was impressed — not only by the way she handled herself in garments that would have trapped and tripped a 21st century hiker, but by her knowledge of the wood. How she found a path, I'll never know, but find one she did. And eventually the four of us stood on the edge of the hidden ravine, just as she'd described it.

I looked with misgiving at the steep downward slant. "Where's the dagger?"

"Hidden, from this side," she said. A smile lifted the corners of her mouth. "But I know where it is."

Rune looked at her with new respect. "You climbed out of this and made it to the highway while you were in labor?"

She laughed. "Needs must when the devil drives."

"Whatever that means," I muttered.

"It's an old saying," said Rune. "It means that when you're in trouble, you do whatever you have to do."

"Right. I knew that."

"Liar," said Lance.

"Shut up," I said. "Man, wholesoul sucks."

Everyone laughed. And then we started the slow and treacherous climb down the ravine.

"Up will be easier than down," Raina assured us when we reached the floor.

"Much," Lance said. "Because I, for one, am going to skatch to the top."

"Good idea, captain," I said, brushing dirt and detritus off my hands and onto my jeans. "It's not like there's a crowd of observers."

"There's my dagger," said Raina, pointing. A small dagger, silver tarnished black, jutted from a high point on the ground. "Open the box."

Lance set the box—muddy now, from sliding most of the way downhill—on a nearby stone and pulled the flaps up. "I dare not approach the dagger, lest I vanish," said Raina. She held out a small spray can of Rustoleum metallic paint: Apple Red. "Lance, would you do the honors?"

He grinned. "I've never been a tagger, but I'll give it my best shot."

"Just a little," warned Rune. "And take care that it can't be seen from above."

Lance shook the can, thinking. "Everybody stand back," he said. We did. About twenty feet north of where we stood, a large chunk of granite stuck out from the side of the ravine. He carefully, and thoroughly, painted its underside metallic Apple Red. He then came back and gave each tree that ringed the dagger a single squirt, about six inches above the root line.

"I don't know if the trees will keep it," he said. "But if they do, you'll be able to guess the year by how high off the ground the dot is. Figuring the trees grow several inches in a year." He jerked his chin at the shiny red rock. "That marker will stay a hundred years unless the rock falls. Maybe longer."

"Would that the paint were visible at night," said Raina. "But that can't be helped."

"Never mind," I said. "You shouldn't try to climb out of here in the dark anyway."

I helped her pack her pockets. She was pretty excited about the gear we'd found. In one pocket, we stuffed a hand-crank/solar LED lantern. We stuck some toothbrushes in around it. The other pocket held two LED flashlights (also of the hand-crank/solar variety), a magnesium fire starter, a big bottle of aspirin, a roll of duct tape and a LifeStraw. The LifeStraw was pretty interesting; I'd never seen one before. It filters water so you can drink out of creeks without poisoning yourself.

When we were done, her skirts were sagging with the weight of it all.

"I've something for you," she said to me, and suddenly her eyes filled with tears. She brushed them away, laughing self-consciously, then reached up and carefully removed the silver circlet from her hair. She placed it on my head. It fit perfectly. Her smile trembled a bit. "Wear it on your wedding day," she whispered. "Will you do that for me?"

I felt my cheeks growing hot. It was difficult to speak past the constriction in my throat, but I managed to croak out, "Yes. Of course. Thank you."

Her warm hands framed my face, and she leaned in to kiss my forehead, then each cheek, lightly. I saw her lips move as she mouthed a blessing, or a prayer. "Farewell then, my little one. Until we meet again."

"Will we meet again?"

The fingers cupping my face shook a little. Another tear spilled down her face. "I pray we will, Zara. On this side of the Great Divide." Her thumbs moved, and I realized she was wiping tears off my cheeks. I guess I was crying too.

"Will you try to come back?"

"I will. I surely will."

We both knew it was a dicey proposition at best.

She turned to go, and Lance—who had been keeping a respectful distance from my brain while all this was going on—shot me a warning. "Wait," I cried. "I almost forgot."

Thank you, Lance. I fumbled in my jacket pocket and drew out an envelope. "This is for you."

Raina took it from my fingers and opened it. Her hazel eyes widened as she peeked inside. "Oh," she breathed. "Oh, this is wonderful. Perfect."

It was, of course, a small packet of photographs— mostly school pictures. The ones I deemed decent enough to copy. First grade, fifth grade, my middle school graduation portrait. My tenth birthday. One from last summer. And the most recent ones, two different shots of me all princessed-up for the homecoming dance a few weeks ago. Felt like ages ago.

I held out my hand for Lance's phone. He gave it to me. "Selfie time," I said. Raina looked at me, uncomprehending. "Like this," I told her, and we mopped up our faces and took a few selfies together, there in the woods. She was amazed.

"I wish I could have a copy of those," she said, smiling as she reviewed them. It looked very odd to see an eighteenth-century woman standing in the forest, flicking through photos on a smartphone. "I'll have to remember, and view them in my mind's eye."

Raina handed the phone back to Lance and shook his hand. "Farewell, Lance," she said. Her eyes crinkled as she looked up at him. "Take good care of my daughter."

His slow smile made him look sly and confident at the same time. "I'll look after her," he said, and tapped his heart with his fist. "That's a promise."

As if I needed looking after. I glowered at him. "Thanks, buddy," I said. "I'll look after you too."

"You're so touchy," he remarked. But he draped his arm across my shoulders and I felt better.

Raina reached out to shake Rune's hand. "Thank you," she said simply.

"You're welcome." Rune covered her hand with his. "I'm sorry to see you go. There's much more I'd like to learn from you."

She patted his hand serenely. "It's well," she said. "You have learned much. Pass your knowledge to the Council and be content."

"That I will," he said, and let her go.

She slipped my envelope of photographs inside her chemise and retied her corset strings over it. "This," she said, patting the packet and laughing a little, "I would be loath to misplace." And with one last, long look at my face — as if she were memorizing it — she took a deep breath and walked toward the dagger.

I've seen some strange stuff in my life — most of it brought on by me — but this was possibly the strangest. Raina Wilder disappeared the way a dust bunny disappears when you come at it with a vacuum cleaner. It was like she was *sucked* into the invisible wormhole. For the tiniest flash of time, we saw her being pulled, and then she was gone. Just gone. In the blink of an eye.

There was a moment of stunned silence, in which we heard the distant drumming of a woodpecker. The ancient trees stood round us, unmoved. No breath of wind stirred in her wake. She was there, and then she was not, with nothing to mark her passage. Rune moved forward as if walking in a dream, and reached his arms into the place where she had stood. Nothing happened. He stepped in. He stepped out. He walked all around it. He walked through it, first in one direction, then another.

"What does it feel like?" Lance asked.

He shook his head, bemused. "Nothing. I feel nothing at all. It's like she skatched, but that's impossible."

"Let me try," I said, and started forward.

"No," said Lance sharply. His hand closed around my wrist. "You're half stick."

The reminder gave me a kind of queasy feeling. "You think it might work on me? I might…vanish?"

"I'd rather not find out," he said grimly. "Humor me."

For once, I was happy to do that.

We put the can of paint back in the box. "What will your report to the Council say?" I asked Rune.

"It'll say that woman is a time traveler," he said. "No doubt in my mind."

"So that means I am who she says I am."

"Yep. No reason to doubt it."

I peeped up at Lance, uncertain of what he was thinking. "That's good, right?"

He relaxed a little and let me into his head. *It's all good, princess.*

I snorted. "I'm not a princess."

"Then take off that crown."

I'd forgotten I was wearing Raina's circlet. "I like it," I said. "I've been thinking about updating my look."

"Backdating your look," he said, correcting me. "That thing is beyond old school. Way beyond."

I knew he thought it was beautiful, so the razzing didn't bother me a bit. "Let's go," I said. "Race you to the top."

"I win," he said from the top of the ravine. I forgot he was going to skatch.

Chapter 16

"Path One," I said, closing my eyes against the sun. I was lying with my head on Lance's thigh. We were stretched on a slab of granite, soaking up the late-autumn sunshine. The rock was surprisingly comfortable, and the day was deliciously warm. "Deny your destiny, suppress your powers, and blend in with the sticks as best you can."

"No thanks," said Lance. "What else you got?"

"Path Two. Go full spellspinner. Trust no one. Split your life between Spellhaven and whatever hidey-hole you carve out for yourself. No family, no friends, no ties of any kind. You're ruled by the Council because the Council's all you have."

"That's more like it."

I opened my eyes and pretended to punch him. He caught my fist and kissed it.

"Path Two is just as bad as Path One."

"Okay," he said. "What's Path Three?"

"I'm not sure, but I think we're on it."

"Yeah? I'm diggin' it so far." He picked up the jacket he'd discarded earlier, folded it, and stuck it behind his head. "Let's stay on Path Three."

"Suits me," I said, yawning. Sunshine always makes me sleepy. "We'll blaze our own trail."

"If it's a good one, others will follow it after us."

"Um-hmm. We'll be pioneers. Whoopee-ti-yi-yo."

"That's a cowboy song."

"Whatever."

A jay zoomed through the redwoods, squawking its wild, woodsy cry. I closed my eyes again and smiled. Life was good today. Peaceful. I was starting to like Spellhaven.

"Do you think they'll let me finish high school?"

"No. You'll have to get your G.E.D." He felt my sadness and gave my hair a gentle tug. "Come on, Zara. You were miserable at that school. The mean girls called you 'Spook.'"

I sighed. "I just wanted so much to be normal."

"You mean Nonny wanted you to be normal."

I thought about it. "You're right."

"I'm always right, babe."

This time I did punch him. He laughed and grabbed me, rolling me onto my back on the rock. "Ow," I said. A pointy bit was digging into my shoulder. He eased my shoulder off the pointy bit and kissed me. The sun and the rock and the kiss and the blue jay...Path Three was definitely my favorite.

My life was much better with Amber under house arrest. Plus the Council had made a few decisions I actually liked. She was going to have the next spellspinner baby, but not with Lance. They were matching her with Evan Doyle, much to Pearl Doyle's delight. So Amber was gearing up to have a little Doyle next July. The Council had spellbound her, removing her ability to skatch, so she was basically going to be at Spellhaven for at least the next year. That suited me just fine. If and when they let her go, she wouldn't be able to touch me or Lance anyway, so I didn't really care how long her sentence turned out to be.

Amber hated being imprisoned here almost as much as I had. Spellhaven didn't give her talents any scope. There was no one to impress, no one to seduce, and—as far as she was concerned—nothing to do. Amber's idea of a good time involved some combination of limousines, dancing, shopping, and alcohol. All of these basic elements were in short supply at Spellhaven.

I'd feel sorry for her, but...nah.

Meanwhile, thanks to Raina's influence on Rune, the Council was rethinking the entire charter of spellspinner rules. A lot of it would doubtless remain the same. Secrecy is always a good idea if you have magical powers. But in light of Amber's recent conduct—which, I gathered, wasn't exactly unique in spellspinner history—the Council was going to revisit its customs regarding child-rearing, at the very least.

They were going to need a fresh path. How lucky for them, that Lance and I were already exploring one.

"So what is Path Three?" I asked, as we made our way back down to the others. Dusk falls quickly in the forest, so we left when the sun touched the top of the trees. "How will our life be different?"

"We'll have each other," said Lance. "That's different."

"But will we live like sticks or like spellspinners?"

"Both." He held a branch up, so I could pass under it without getting smacked in the face. "Neither. We'll have the best of both worlds. What do you like most about the stick world?"

"Home," I said at once. "We'll have friends. Not many, but a few. And if we have a family, we won't scatter and live apart. We'll stay together, like a stick family."

I felt the doubts in the back of Lance's mind, and squeezed his hand. "You'll love it. And we won't run any stupid risks. We'll live in the country. That's what I'm used to anyhow, so I won't mind. It'll be almost like the loner thing you're used to, except you won't be alone."

The well-hidden cabins of Spellhaven were visible now, lamplit windows glimmering through the forest. Looking through Lance's eyes, Spellhaven at close of day was cozy and welcoming. Safe. Homelike, I realized. This was where he'd spent most of his childhood. It had been a lonely childhood, but filled with beauty too.

"And we'll have Spellhaven," I promised. "We'll always have Spellhaven."

They had given me my own skatching stone. It wasn't, like everyone else's, the stone where I was born.

Duh. But it was a safe place that would always be kept empty, waiting for me. In any emergency, I would have a place to go.

It had been Nedra Wilder's stone. They held a special ceremony, with everyone present—even Amber, though she was forced to stand in the back. Rune had gently smoothed his hand over Nedra's name and it had vanished. Now the stone said simply, WILDER. I told them that would do, for now. It didn't feel right to carve ZARA on it, when I'd been born in a hospital miles from here.

I spent quite a bit of time on that stone, thinking. And letting the place sink into my subconscious, so I could call it up in a snap and skatch to it. I practiced, a time or two—I went home to have dinner with Nonny and sleep in my own bed, then skatched back to my stone in the morning. Easy-peasy.

I loved having my own skatching stone. When I sat on my stone among all the other stones that dotted the grass like irregular pavement, I felt truly connected to my father's people for the first time.

Lance picked up on my thoughts and smiled. "You like it now."

"Spellhaven?" I waved my arm, vaguely encompassing the scene. "It has a certain rustic charm."

"Careful, Zara. You'll be a right spellspinner before you know it."

I laughed to hear him echoing Raina's words. And I didn't say it aloud, but I knew he was wrong. I didn't expect to ever fit perfectly in either world. I was too much a stick to fit in here, with my father's fey, half-wild kinsmen. And so much a spellspinner that I'd never fit in among sticks.

But I was at peace with it now. I liked having a foot in each world. They were both great, in their own way, and I didn't mind my new role: a bridge between the people and places I loved.

"Change is in the air," I said, with a sense of satisfaction.

Lance sniffed, then shook his head. "Nah. That's lighter fluid. Somebody's starting up the barbecue."

"What's for dinner tonight?"

"Beats me."

I grabbed his hand. "Let's go find out. Because, you know, the time for secrets is past." And laughing, we half-ran, half-skidded down the hill toward the dining hall.

 Diane Farr was first published at the age of eight when the local newspaper printed one of her poems. She has spent most of her life with her nose in a book -- sometimes reading, sometimes writing. Eventually she produced eight historical romances and a novella, all published by Signet Books. Diane lives in Northern California with two cats and a husband. You can learn more about her books at dianefarrbooks.com. She'd be happy to hear from you on Twitter or Facebook:

Twitter: @DianeFarr

Facebook: facebook.com/dianefarrpage

Made in the USA
Columbia, SC
01 September 2021

44434515R00104